Death by Golf

by Gregg Kreutz

A SAMUEL FRENCH ACTING EDITION

SAMUEL FRENCH

FOUNDED 1830

NEW YORK HOLLYWOOD LONDON TORONTO

SAMUELFRENCH.COM

ISBN 978-0-573-69943-6   Printed in U.S.A.   #29857

MUSIC USE NOTE

Licensees are solely responsible for obtaining formal written permission from copyright owners to use copyrighted music in the performance of this play and are strongly cautioned to do so. If no such permission is obtained by the licensee, then the licensee must use only original music that the licensee owns and controls. Licensees are solely responsible and liable for all music clearances and shall indemnify the copyright owners of the play and their licensing agent, Samuel French, Inc., against any costs, expenses, losses and liabilities arising from the use of music by licensees.

IMPORTANT BILLING AND CREDIT REQUIREMENTS

All producers of *DEATH BY GOLF* must give credit to the Author of the Play in all programs distributed in connection with performances of the Play, and in all instances in which the title of the Play appears for the purposes of advertising, publicizing or otherwise exploiting the Play and/or a production. The name of the Author *must* appear on a separate line on which no other name appears, immediately following the title and *must* appear in size of type not less than fifty percent of the size of the title type.

DEATH BY GOLF was first produced at the Pioneer Playhouse in Danville, Kentucky on August 10, 2005. The performance was produced by Charlotte Henson and directed by Holly Henson. The cast was as follows:

GRANDPA	Dave Haller
ASHLEY	Laura Riley
MURIEL	Patricia Hammond
TONY	Robert Hess, Jr.
PRESCOTT	Robert Hess, Jr.

CHARACTERS

GRANDPA – Scrappy old-timer. A good hearted soul who's not as befuddled as he at first appears.

ASHLEY – A little frantic, a little impulsive. She's bright, but life has pushed her around so much that her judgement's questionable.

MURIEL – A serious-minded attorney, not above looking out for number one.

TONY – Subject of a five-state manhunt. Anxious.

PRESCOTT – Articulate, resourceful, charming, homicidal. He's become manically obsessed with hitting it big.

SETTING

The Interior of Grandpa's comfortably dilapidated North Florida bungalow. There's a fair amount of golf debris scattered about – trophies, bags, clubs – in addition to some tropical plants and a birdcage. On the back wall Grandpa has hung a "WELCOME NEWLYWEDS" sign. Stage right has a front door and a window, stage left has a window, a bathroom door, and a back door. Upstage from right to left is the stairway to the upstairs, the center stage closet, and a somewhat low-tech kitchen featuring refrigerator, cabinets, counter, and gas stove. A well-used (possibly bamboo) couch and a rickety table-and-chair-set complete the scene.

ACT ONE

(GRANDPA is facing the stage right window, poised over a golf ball that's teed up on the floor. Gripping the club, arms stretched behind him, he's getting ready for the big swing. Just as he's about to unleash, he pauses, then lowers the club, steps away from the ball, goes over to the window and – so that the ball won't break anything – opens the window. Then he returns to the ball and gets into position again. He is maneuvering himself into full swing mode when, unheard by him, there is knocking at the door.)

MURIEL. *(offstage) (Knock knock)* Hello? Hello?

(More knocking. Opening the door and sticking her head in.)

Hello? Anybody home?

(seeing **GRANDPA** *– his back to her – she enters.)*

Hello. Hello.

(When preoccupied **GRANDPA** *still doesn't respond, she goes up to him.)*

Excuse me...

(GRANDPA is getting more and more involved with setting up for the swing. Now full volume.)

EXCUSE ME.

GRANDPA. *(Startled. Dropping his arms. Turning and gasping a little.)* Ooo, you gave me a start! Just about scared me out of my wits.

MURIEL. Sorry.

GRANDPA. Such as they are.

MURIEL. I was knocking for a while.

7

GRANDPA. Well, I'm not saying I really mind or anything, but next time, if you like, you could try knocking.

MURIEL. I did knock quite a bit.

GRANDPA. But heck, I don't care really either way. Knock or don't knock. It's just that if you scared me real bad and I dropped dead you'd feel responsible. I don't want you to come over for a friendly visit or whatever it is you're here for, and then spend the rest of your life tortured by guilt.

MURIEL. I knocked.

GRANDPA. What's that?

MURIEL. I knocked.

GRANDPA. I'm sorry. One more time.

(**MURIEL** *goes back to the door and pounds on it –
KNOCK KNOCK KNOCK – as she says…*)

I knocked!

GRANDPA. Well, it's a little late for that now.

MURIEL. Are you Mr. Deemer?

GRANDPA. Come again?

MURIEL. ARE YOU MR. DEEMER?

GRANDPA. That's right. And who are you?

MURIEL. *(rapidly)* I'm Muriel Carlan and I'm terribly sorry for just barging in like this but on the car radio all anyone can seem to talk about is this escaped prisoner and I'm afraid it's gotten me a little rattled having to constantly hear "Murderer on the loose." And "Slasher Killer escapes" and all that.

GRANDPA. Just a tad louder.

MURIEL. *(a little louder)* And with all these sightings in the area I was concerned that standing around out there on the porch might be a prelude to me becoming the actual *(cringing smile)* "next victim."

GRANDPA. You know what? I should have told you right away; my hearing aid's concked out. You're gonna have to speak up quite a bit.

MURIEL. *(louder still)* I was saying that when I knocked and you didn't answer, I was a little anxious because of the escaped convict which is why I came right in.

GRANDPA. What's that?

MURIEL. *(still louder)* Because of the convict I came right in.

GRANDPA. You what?

MURIEL. *(yelling)* I CAME RIGHT IN!

GRANDPA. *(also yelling)* I NOTICED.

MURIEL. And the reason I came in was because of the escaped...

GRANDPA. *(tapping his hearing aid)* Sorry to interrupt, but I'm not gettin much of a signal from this old thing-a-ma-jig. You don't happen to have any hearing aid repair tools do you?

MURIEL. I don't think so. Let me see.

(looks in her purse and pulls out a fairly big brightly colored nail file)

Nail file?

GRANDPA. *(peering at it then shaking his head)* Too big. See I happen to have a very teeny tiny little doo hinkie.

(Pause while he considers what this might sound like. Pointing at Muriel.)

Hearing aid.

MURIEL. Yes.

GRANDPA. *(taking it out of his ear and shaking it, then putting it back)* And it's a shame cause this darn hoozit was working like a charm yesterday. Clear as a bell. Wonder what happened.

MURIEL. Mr. Deemer, the reason I've come here today is because...

GRANDPA. Wait; I got an idea! Hold on now.

(goes to the open closet and starts rummaging)

Let's get some technical assistance. I got something in this old closet that might solve the problem.

(rumages around in the closet)

GRANDPA. *(cont.)* Just a second.

> *(Finds the megaphone and brings it out. Holding it up.)*

Here try this.

> *(After a pause,* **MURIEL** *goes up to him, takes the mega-phone, and carries it dubiously back downstage.)*

See if that'll help.

> *(***GRANDPA*** *then reaches out and – facing stage left so he doesn't notice anything unusual – closes the closet door. Then he heads over the* **MURIEL**. *The door closing reveals* **TONY** *[The escaped convict] who's been pressed against the wall behind the door. He is scary-looking, dressed in a torn orange prison jump suit, and holding Grandpa's knife but neither* **GRANDPA** *nor* **MURIEL** *see him. During the following,* **TONY** *quietly reopens the closet door, goes in the closet, and shuts the door.)*

> *(joining Muriel)* Okay; give her a try.

MURIEL. *(reluctantly lifting it to her lips and pushing the button.)* Mr. Deemer?

GRANDPA. Yes.

MURIEL. As I said, my name is Muriel Carlan and I've been looking for you for quite a while.

GRANDPA. You have?

MURIEL. All over the Southeast as a matter of fact. Pensacola, Tempe, Risco. Finally someone in town knew you and gave me directions. But it took at least an hour to locate that little turn off road into the woods here. You're a difficult person to find.

GRANDPA. I didn't know that. Interesting. Course you may be one of the few that's ever actually tried to find me. Far as I know that isn't too common an activity. *(gesturing to the table)* Here, have a seat. *(as they sit down)* The rest of the world doesn't seem to feel that urge very often. I could be wrong though. Maybe there's all sorts of people out there desperate to locate me and just unable to do it. How would I ever know? There might be just giant hoards of eager people hunting around for me all over the countryside and being thwarted by...

MURIEL. Mr. Deemer

GRANDPA. Yes'm.

MURIEL. I need to talk to you.

GRANDPA. Okay.

MURIEL. I've been looking for you for a reason.

GRANDPA. I see.

MURIEL. I am an attorney.

GRANDPA. Oh-oh.

MURIEL. And I've come here today to tell you something important.

GRANDPA. Okay.

MURIEL. I've come to tell you about a significant amount of money.

GRANDPA. Well, I may as well warn you, I'm on a limited income and I would love to help out but right now I'm a little short.

MURIEL. No, you don't understand; *you* would be getting the money.

GRANDPA. Well that's the problem, I don't know where I would be getting the money from.

MURIEL. Mr. Deemer, there is a complicated legal inheritance situation that I need to explain to you and I want to make sure you fully understand it.

GRANDPA. Good luck.

MURIEL. But it doesn't only involve you. It also involves your granddaughter.

GRANDPA. Ashley?

MURIEL. That's right. Ashley Deemer.

GRANDPA. Well, that's a break for you. She's coming up here this afternoon.

MURIEL. *(putting the megaphone down and talking normally)* When?

GRANDPA. What's that?

MURIEL. *(using the megaphone again)* When?

GRANDPA. Maybe in an hour or so.

MURIEL. An hour?

GRANDPA. Or so. She's coming up from Fort Lauderdale. That's where the cruise ship docked. She's gotten herself a job on one of those cruise ships they have down there as the ping pong coordinator. She goes all over the Caribbean and helps people with their ping pong.

MURIEL. Well that actually is quite fortuitous because I do want to meet her.

GRANDPA. And you'll get to meet her new husband too. Percival or Peterson or, I know, Prescott. That's his name. He's driving down from Savannah. They just got married you know.

MURIEL. I didn't know that.

GRANDPA. Only about three weeks ago. *(gesturing towards the banner)* See?

MURIEL. *(looking at the banner)* Ah hah.

GRANDPA. Here look. *(grabbing a framed clipping off a table)* Here's the announcement from the paper.

(She looks at it.)

Isn't she pretty? And then right after the wedding, Ashley had to rush off and do her little cruise job. They haven't even had their honeymoon yet.

MURIEL. *(handing back the clipping)* Why didn't he go on the cruise with her?

GRANDPA. Sea sick. So this is great. They'll be here soon and in the meantime you and I can just sit back and relax and you can yell things at me through the megaphone.

MURIEL. *(putting down the megaphone)* I don't know if I can stand to do that any more.

GRANDPA. Excuse me?

MURIEL. *(now through the megaphone)* I'm saying I don't know if I can stand to talk through this thing any more.

GRANDPA. Oh dear. Is it kind of irritating?

MURIEL. Yes.

GRANDPA. Well, try without it. Just speak very clearly.

MURIEL. *(strong enunciation)* WHAT DOES ASHLEY'S HUSBAND DO FOR A LIVING?

GRANDPA. *(also over-enunciating)* I'M NOT SURE. MAYBE SOMETHING TO DO WITH GEOMETRY.

MURIEL. GEOMETRY?

GRANDPA. YES, HE'S MAYBE A GEOMETRIST.

MURIEL. I DON'T THINK THAT'S A REAL PROFESSION.

GRANDPA. DON'T TELL *HIM* THAT.

MURIEL. WHY ARE YOU TALKING THIS WAY?

GRANDPA. TALKING WHICH WAY?

MURIEL. THIS WAY.

GRANDPA. I DON'T WANT YOU TO FEEL STRANGE.

MURIEL. *(picking up megaphone)* Mr. Deemer, this is quite important, actually very important; do you think you could possibly try to listen to me for one moment. I need very badly to tell you some vital information about a significant amount of money and I would really appreciate having your full attention.

(pause)

GRANDPA. *(snapping fingers)* Earwax!

MURIEL. Excuse me?

GRANDPA. Earwax! I bet that's what's causing the trouble. This little watch-a-ma-call-it's gotten itself all clogged up.

*(**GRANDPA** takes it out of his ear, blows on it a little while to heat it up and loosen up the wax, puts it in his mouth, and sucks. Then he leans over the waste basket and spits. Then more blowing sucking and spitting. **MURIEL** watches this unsightly activity with a slightly queazy expression.)*

Sorry about this.

(When he's finally done he puts it back in his ear.)

Now let's see if we can get some reception. Give her a try; say something.

MURIEL. I feel sick?

GRANDPA. Well what do you know; clear as crystal.

MURIEL. Good.

GRANDPA. Now tell me what you need all the money for.

MURIEL. No, you see I don't need money. Well, I need money. That's true. I could certainly use some money. But not the kind of money you're thinking of. The money I'm concerned with is huge money. Perhaps millions of dollars. And that's why it's so important that I come here in person and, if possible, have your complete attention while I tell you about it.

GRANDPA. Okay?

MURIEL. First of all I wasn't asking you to give me money.

GRANDPA. Good. I don't have any.

MURIEL. I was trying to *tell* you about money.

GRANDPA. No need to. I know all about it. The root of all evil. Fact, show me a man with a lot of money and I'll show you someone with a double digit handicap.

MURIEL. What I wanted to talk to you about is not money in general, but money that might be directly connected to you.

GRANDPA. You're barking up the wrong tree little lady. I haven't seen anything bigger than a twenty dollar bill since I bet on Jack Nicklas in 1962.

MURIEL. Now listen. This is important. A lot depends on this. There's a time factor. I've been trying to find you for a long time. There's an inheritance. A big inheritance. A lot of money. Do you understand, a lot of money.

GRANDPA. That's just what I made when he won it. Nicklas. A lot of money. I spent it all on golf clubs though.

MURIEL. *(with mounting intensity)* This is more than that. This isn't just golf club money. With this money you could buy golf clubs to circle your house. You could pave your driveway with golf clubs. You could have golf club tables and golf club chandeliers and make a four poster bed out of golf clubs. And when you were done with that you could buy some real golf clubs that YOU COULD PLAY GOLF IN! DO YOU UNDERSTAND?!

GRANDPA. Has anyone ever told you you're a little preoccupied with golf?

MURIEL. *(Pause. Trying to compose herself.)* Mr. Deemer, I have something important to tell you, but maybe it'll be easier for both of us, if before we get to that, you answered some questions.

GRANDPA. *(straightening up in his chair)* Fire away.

MURIEL. First of all, I'm wondering if there's any chance that you still have your original birth certificate.

GRANDPA. Birth certificate? Well, that's funny.

MURIEL. What?

GRANDPA. Ashley told me on the phone that her new husband is hoping I still have my birth certificate. Said he's wanting to look at it.

MURIEL. Really?

GRANDPA. Yep, she asked me if I could try to dig it up.

MURIEL. *He* wanted to see it?

GRANDPA. That's right.

MURIEL. And did Ashley tell you why?

GRANDPA. Not that I noticed.

MURIEL. Strange. You know, all of a sudden, I'm interested in that new husband.

GRANDPA. What do you mean?

MURIEL. I think I'm actually very interested in him.

GRANDPA. Careful, he's a married man.

MURIEL. I can't imagine why was he wanting your birth certificate.

GRANDPA. *(rising)* Who knows, but maybe while we're chatting, I should try and hunt it down.

MURIEL. Where do you think it is?

GRANDPA. *(heading towards the closet)* I got a pretty good idea it's somewhere in that closet.

MURIEL. And when is the new husband supposed to arrive?

GRANDPA. What's that?

MURIEL. When is he supposed to arrive?

GRANDPA. Maybe in an hour.

MURIEL. Because I would love to find out from him what exactly he needs it for.

GRANDPA. *(hand on knob, about to open the closet door)* Oops. I'm losing you. Could you try that again a little louder?

MURIEL. *(louder)* I would love to find out what he needs it for.

GRANDPA. Damn.

(pointing at his ear)

Off again.

(letting go of the knob and heading back to the table where **MURIEL** *'s sitting)*

I'm afraid there's no way around it,

(pulling the hearing aid out of his ear)

We need to do another treatment.

(He starts blowing on it.)

MURIEL. *(Groaning at the prospect of watching the process again, she stands up in alarm.)* You know what? I think I'm going to go now and come back when Ashley and her husband are here.

(heading for the front door)

So thanks so much Mr. Deemer and I'll see you again very shortly.

(She opens the door, scans quickly to see if there are any convicts around and exits.)

GRANDPA. *(starting to follow her)* Oh. Okay. Bye.

(calling out:) OR MAYBE HE'S A GENETISIST.

(He goes back to the table, blows on the hearing aid, sucks on it, spits out some wax, repeats a few times and then puts the devise back in his ear. He suddenly notices the ball still on its tee on the floor. He goes over to it, picks up the club, and is just getting back into position when…)

ASHLEY. *(calling from outside)* SAND TRAP!!

GRANDPA. What's that?

ASHLEY. SAND TRAP!!

GRANDPA. *(looking around trying to track where the sound is coming from)* Sand trap, sand trap.

ASHLEY. SAND TRAP!!

GRANDPA. *(Looking around some more. Finally going to the window.)* Oh my Lord. Ashley! Our distress signal.

(leaning out the window)

Ashley? Ashley?

ASHLEY. Grandpa!

GRANDPA. What are you doing out there? Why are you saying sand trap?

ASHLEY. I've been having a tough time.

GRANDPA. Well, get in here for heaven's sake.

(Opens the back door. **ASHLEY** *enters.)*

ASHLEY. *(on the verge of tears)* Oh, Grandpa!

(They hug.)

GRANDPA. Ashley, sweetheart. Oh my goodness. What's going on. What are you doing out there yelling sand trap?

(looking out the window)

And where's your car?

ASHLEY. I didn't drive.

GRANDPA. So how'd you get up here?

ASHLEY. That's the thing; since Prescott's driving down I didn't want us to have two cars. And then, you see, this man, on the ship – one of the passengers – he said he was coming up this way and he'd be happy to give me a ride.

GRANDPA. Oh. Well where is he?

ASHLEY. The man?

GRANDPA. Yes.

ASHLEY. I think he might be in the hospital.

GRANDPA. Why is he in the hospital?

ASHLEY. Grandpa, he got a little fresh with me and I'm afraid, well, I'm afraid I may have broken his nose.

GRANDPA. How?

ASHLEY. *(holding up a ping pong paddle)* It could of been bad cause he was kind of aggressive, but luckily it happened near the turn off right out there so I was able to smash him and get out of the car and scramble through the woods here which I didn't like too much cause of the bugs and the escapee business but as it happened I made it through without any real difficulties.

(close to tears) So it was not really a problem.

(She breaks down and hugs him again.)

Oh, Grandpa.

(calming down a little) If you don't mind though, come to think of it, maybe don't let's tell Prescott when he gets here about me and the driver of the car and the nose and the hospital and everything. Why don't we just say I took a limo?

GRANDPA. But why didn't you take a limo?

ASHLEY. I don't know. After that big wedding expense, I don't feel like I ever want to spend any money again.

GRANDPA. I would have been so happy to pay for a limo.

ASHLEY. Grandpa, you don't have any money.

GRANDPA. I got enough to keep my granddaughter from getting molested on the highway.

(He goes to a side table, pulls a gun out of the drawer, and heads to the door.)

ASHLEY. What are you doing?

GRANDPA. I'll be right back.

ASHLEY. Why do you have that gun?

GRANDPA. I'm off to the hospital.

ASHLEY. Grandpa, stop that! Put that thing back in the drawer! Right this instant! I mean it!

GRANDPA. Just a quick visit.

ASHLEY. In the drawer! I can't believe you would even think of doing such a thing. You can't behave that way; you've got a heart condition.

GRANDPA. *(as he puts it back)* I just thought maybe I could give him a heart condition too.

ASHLEY. And don't ever get that out again. Understand?

GRANDPA. All right.

ASHLEY. I mean it! There. That's better. Grandpa, you've got to settle down. Okay?

GRANDPA. Okay.

ASHLEY. Now! Like the doctor said, you've got to keep from getting all agitated. *(Notices bird. Screams.)* Ahh!!

GRANDPA. *(agitated)* What?!

ASHLEY. Freckles!! *(She rushes over to the cage.)* Oh my God, Freckles! He looks completely healed!

GRANDPA. Well, I been taking good care of him.

ASHLEY. His wing looks so much better! *(to Freckles)* Aren't you better, Freckles? Yes, you are. Yes, you are. *(to* **GRANDPA***)* So that little splint you made worked?

GRANDPA. Seems like it.

ASHLEY. *(to bird)* You are such a lucky bird that Grandpa found you out there. He completely healed your little broken bone didn't he? *(to* **GRANDPA***)* See Grandpa, that's why I want you to meet Prescott.

GRANDPA. Why, did he break something?

ASHLEY. No, but he is also a very caring person. I think you're just going to love him.

GRANDPA. I'm sure I will. You know this will be the first time I've ever met a professional geologist.

ASHLEY. Genealogist, Grandpa. He does genealogy. Oh you're going to be so interested. He can track down people's roots and family trees and figure out who's related to who and all that kind of thing. He's so good at it. He knows all about my background and your background, too. He says we come from very interesting stock.

GRANDPA. Well we do. I understand there's a great uncle somewhere back there who they say may have once held down a real job.

ASHLEY. Grandpa, you've held down real jobs.

GRANDPA. Just golf jobs. Teaching or coaching or selling equipment or doing little side-bets. I don't think anybody would confuse any of that with working.

ASHLEY. Just cause you enjoy it doesn't mean it's not work.

GRANDPA. Yeah, I think it does. It's all moot now though. I'm kind of washed up.

ASHLEY. What do you mean?

GRANDPA. I mean I've lost my stroke.

ASHLEY. What stroke?

GRANDPA. My big swing. It's gone. I can't get my arms back to parallel.

ASHLEY. You'll get it back.

GRANDPA. I don't know sweetheart, from now on *(bending for a simulated miniature golf stroke)* it might be just putt-putt through the windmills. But listen, what can I get for you. You want some coffee or iced tea or anything?

ASHLEY. No, I want to go fix myself up for when Prescott arrives. *(She looks in the mirror and primps.)*

GRANDPA. *(also looking in the mirror and primping)* Me too.

ASHLEY. Listen, Grandpa, can I ask you something?

GRANDPA. Yes?

ASHLEY. Um..well... *(suddenly taking her glasses off)* Do you think I look better without glasses?

GRANDPA. Honey, you look good with 'em or without.

ASHLEY. I want Prescott to see me at my best.

GRANDPA. I wouldn't worry about it. Either way he's hit the jackpot.

ASHLEY. So should I leave them off?

GRANDPA. *(After patting down his few hairs he moves away from the mirror.)* They do say in marriage the less well you see the better.

ASHLEY. All right, off. *(She goes and puts them on the counter.)* And speaking of marriage Grandpa, *(She turns towards where Grandpa was just standing.)* I um…I wanted to ask you about something.

GRANDPA. Over here.

ASHLEY. *(turning to where he's now standing)* Oh.

(joining him)

Grandpa, do you think it's normal to be a little scared when you start out in marriage?

(They both sit down on the couch.)

GRANDPA. Well, sure. I remember I was absolutely terrified when I first got married.

ASHLEY. You were?

GRANDPA. Petrified. Conversationally my first wife tended to go on and on all day long and I was scared to death that the only time I was going to get any peace was when I went to bed. As it happened though I couldn't have been more wrong.

ASHLEY. But were you nervous that you'd maybe rushed into it too quickly?

GRANDPA. Oh sure. I think everybody feels that way. Her dad sure did. I never saw a man take less of a liking to a son-in-law. One time he pulled me aside and said I was a useless, parasitic, aimless, shiftless, brainless golf bum. Imagine; me – brainless.

ASHLEY. Cause Grandpa I've been worried that I'm riding on some crazy runaway train. It's not that I don't love Prescott, I do, and I know that you're going to love him too. But now that I've gone this far, I'm just kind of anxious that the real reason I maybe rushed into this was cause, well, cause *(intensely)* I HATED SO MUCH BEING SINGLE! There, isn't that terrible? But it's true, you have no idea how awful it is to be single.

GRANDPA. Hey wait, I'm single.

ASHLEY. You can't imagine who is out there. The last five years has been like one giant loser parade. All those dinners and drinks and bars and the worst part is when you get taken home and you have to figure out how to avoid getting intimate.

GRANDPA. *(shaking head knowingly) Tell* me about it.

ASHLEY. And it wasn't just that they were losers. So many of them were mean losers. I seemed to be a magnet for unfriendly guys with tattoos on their necks who always seemed to be putting me down. I mean, I don't mind a little of that bad boy stuff, but after a while I wanted to be able to end a relationship without a restraining order. So when Prescott came on the scene all proper and respectable I think I was kind of a sitting duck. Don't get me wrong, I'm not having second thoughts. At all. I mean when you meet Prescott you'll be amazed; he's just about the most interesting man you can imagine.

GRANDPA. I'm sure he is.

ASHLEY. He knows about everything, and he's so curious and he's so involved with all his genealogical investigations. You'll see; you'll be fascinated. And of course naturally when a person's that mentally engaged in so many things of course sometimes they get a little frazzled. A little hot tempered. I mean who wouldn't? They say geniuses often have short fuses. Wasn't Isaac Newton always throwing things at his wife?

GRANDPA. I think that was Wayne Newton.

ASHLEY. So the fact that I'm a little nervous, a little apprehensive about what I've gotten myself into is entirely normal. Isn't that right Grandpa?

GRANDPA. No question about it.

ASHLEY. Good, *(starting to crack)* I feel so much better.

(She sniffles and throws herself into **GRANDPA***'s arms.)*

(through her tears) Oh, Grandpa!

GRANDPA. *(patting her)* Come on. There there. It's okay.

(More sobbing from **ASHLEY.** *Finally...)*

Ashley, are you sure that all this concern about your new marriage isn't because I wasn't able to be at your wedding?

ASHLEY. What? No, don't be silly.

GRANDPA. 'Cause maybe if I'd been there, me being, you know; your one living relative, you would have felt like you were more officially married.

ASHLEY. Oh, Grandpa, That's not it at all. I told you; don't worry that you weren't there. We just had some very bad timing. And plus I know that with your heart condition and everything your doctor said you shouldn't be exposed to situations where you get too excited.

GRANDPA. He should explain that to his nurse.

ASHLEY. But the main thing is; you were there at my wedding in spirit.

GRANDPA. Well, I promise you one thing, whatever happens, however complicated it gets, I guarantee you I won't miss the next one.

ASHLEY. Grandpa!!

GRANDPA. No, I didn't mean that. At all. This is going to be a wonderful marriage and I'm sure your new husband is a wonderful man and you just have to trust me; it's all going to be...wonderful.

ASHLEY. Thanks, Grandpa, you're really sweet. Now let me go get organized for the big arrival.

(goes over to her suitcase and picks it up)

GRANDPA. Hey, let me help you with that.

ASHLEY. No, I've got it, and you know what? *(pulling the gun out of the drawer)* I think I'll just keep this in my purse for the time being. Just so it's out of harm's way.

GRANDPA. Whatever you think.

ASHLEY. *(as she starts up the stairs)* So I'll straighten up and maybe I'll...Oh wait; did you have any luck finding that birth certificate?

GRANDPA. Not yet but I got a good idea where it is.

MURIEL. Well, if you could find it before Prescott gets here that'd be real helpful.

GRANDPA. I'm on the case.

(**ASHLEY** *exits.*)

GRANDPA. *(circling back towards the closet)* Birth certificate. Birth certificate. Birth cer...

(He notices the teed ball on the floor and stops. He picks up the club and starts getting in position. He is just about to give it the full swing when...)

ASHLEY. *(from upstairs)* Any luck yet.

GRANDPA. Just about.

He reluctantly puts down the club and heads towards the closet. As he approaches he points at it and says...)

Closet.

(He opens the door and then backs up when he sees **TONY.** **TONY** *has changed into Grandpa's loud plaid pants and a black polo shirt.)*

(Frozen for a moment while the two men stare at each other. Finally:)

TONY. Surprise!

GRANDPA. Oh my goodness! What in the world?

(Not sure what to think. Then it clicks.)

Wait a second; Perceval?

TONY. Yeah.

GRANDPA. I mean, Prescott!

TONY. ...Yeah.

GRANDPA. Well I'll be! Prescott! My very own grandson in law! Come out here, young man. You rascal. Thought you'd surprise old Grandpa, didn't you?

TONY. Yeah.

GRANDPA. *(pulling him out)* Well, you sure did. That was a good one. I never even had a suspicion someone was there. When'd you go in there?

TONY. Uh…before.

GRANDPA. Well I'll be. Ashley told me you're quite the jokester, but this is a real dandy. I can tell we're going to have some fun around here now. You can just hide inside things and behind things around the house all you want. And there's some nice big trees outside. *(noticing the knife)* Well, lookee there. I can't believe it! My carving knife! I have been looking for that fricken thing for three days. *(taking the knife from **TONY**)* Where was it?

TONY. Over on the ledge there.

GRANDPA. Well isn't that great; we got a finder in the family. You haven't seen the T.V. remote have you?

TONY. No.

GRANDPA. Well, be on the look out.

*(noticing what **TONY**'s wearing)*

Say, those are some good looking pants.

TONY. ….Thank you.

GRANDPA. *(a slight look towards the closet)* I used to have a pair a little like that. Yes sir, you are a fine-looking new husband. Hey now, let me go tell Ashley that her fine looking new husband is here. I'll be right back.

TONY. Wait. Maybe we shouldn't be letting her know I'm here.

GRANDPA. Oh. Of course. You want to surprise her!

TONY. …Maybe.

GRANDPA. Sure you do and I think that's a great idea. Let's give her a big surprise. Okay, now what should we do?

TONY. Maybe I should just head out.

GRANDPA. Head out? Oh you mean so that you can walk back in when she comes down.

TONY. Something like that.

GRANDPA. Well, that doesn't seem like too good a surprise. You just walking in the door. I think we should put you back in the closet.

TONY. No, I really better be getting out of here.

GRANDPA. *(leading* **TONY** *back to the closet and shutting the door)* Just get right back in there. This will really tickle Ashley.

(He puts the knife on the counter then heads for the stairs but notices the door starting to open. He goes and shuts it. It opens again and he shuts it again.)

GRANDPA. Now listen here, Peterson. You don't seem very good at sticking with the program. I want you to stay in....

ASHLEY. *(from upstairs)* Grandpa?

GRANDPA. Yes?

ASHLEY. Are you sure Prescott will be able to find this place?

GRANDPA. *(yelling up to* **ASHLEY***)* Oh he'll find it alright. *(to* **TONY***)* Just calm down okay?.

(shutting the door again)

ASHLEY. Cause you *are* kind of hidden out here in the cypress grove. *(entering)* All these trees everywhere and just that little dirt road up to the house. What if he gets lost?

GRANDPA. Trust me he will not get lost. Now lookee here, Ashley. I've got something I want to show you.

ASHLEY. What?

GRANDPA. *(leading her to in front of the closet)* Over here. I got a surprise. Something you're really going to like.

ASHLEY. What kind of surprise?

GRANDPA. I'm not saying. You just get ready for something very unexpected to pop out of that closet.

(Pause while **GRANDPA** *and* **ASHLEY** *look at the closet door.* **ASHLEY** *grinning in anticipation.)*

Something you're really going to be happy to see.

(pause)

Look out now.

(pause)

A big surprise.

ASHLEY. *(through the grin)* Okay, I'm ready.

(pause)

GRANDPA. We're ready.

(pause)

(GRANDPA goes up to the closet and opens the door.)

Ta da.

(ASHLEY, still grinning, stands in shock staring at TONY for a fairly long pause. Finally she lets out a scream, rushes up to TONY and leaps into his arms.)

ASHLEY. Prescott!! Prescott, you cutie pie. That is so darling, you hiding in that closet. Was that your idea or Grandpa's?

GRANDPA. It was kind of a joint effort.

ASHLEY. Well, that is so adorable. Coming up with a surprise. And what do you think, Grandpa? Have you ever seen a handsomer man?

GRANDPA. Come to think of it, I don't believe I ever have.

ASHLEY. I mean look at him! *(She moves him into better viewing position.)* Take a good look at maybe the handsom... where did you get those pants?

TONY. Oh. These? I...

GRANDPA. What's wrong with those pants?

ASHLEY. Just that they seem to be the ugliest pants I ever saw.

GRANDPA. I think they look good.

ASHLEY. *(to TONY)* Don't tell me you were wearing those out in public.

GRANDPA. Of course he was.

ASHLEY. And nobody shot at you or anything?

GRANDPA. Don't listen to her, Prescott. She just doesn't understand plaid.

ASHLEY. Did you bring another pair?

TONY. Look I...

ASHLEY. Good. We'll get you changed into those and then we can have a ceremonial burning.

GRANDPA. Now listen, I think I'm going to leave you two little love birds alone now.

ASHLEY. No, don't go, Grandpa.

GRANDPA. Come on, I know how it is. Just got married. Haven't seen each other for two weeks. No, I'm gonna go out to my garden now and feed the mosquitoes and see how the weeds are doing. If you need me you know where the path is.

(exits)

ASHLEY. *(leading* **TONY** *over to the couch)* Now, Prescott sweetheart, I want you to tell me everything you've been doing since I last saw you. Every single thing. I want to hear it all from your own lips. From your own handsome lips.

TONY. You know there's something that....

ASHLEY. Wait, first tell me what happened with that job. The family tree thing, okay? That client you didn't like. The horrible woman? Did that go okay?

TONY. Listen what you need to know is that...

ASHLEY. Were you able to research her roots and come up with some embarrassing ancestors for her?

TONY. Ashley I think you better...

ASHLEY. Serial killers or pedophiles or politicians.

TONY. Listen, Ashley, I need to tel.....

ASHLEY. Hey, have you got a cold?

TONY. No?

ASHLEY. Well, you sound kind of different.

TONY. There's a real good reason for that.

ASHLEY. Like your voice is lower.

TONY. I know.

ASHLEY. Poor little baby.

TONY. I want to say that I...

ASHLEY. *(pullling his head onto her chest)* Aw; did you get sick while I was away?

(pause)

TONY. .....Maybe.

ASHLEY. *(stroking his head)* Well, bless your heart you poor little, sick little, husband. There there. Oh my goodness. All alone up in Savannah and nobody to look after you. Now don't you worry. Ashley is here and you are going to be nursed back to health.

TONY. *(coughs)*

ASHLEY. And I've got a special treatment program for you. A special customized caretaking procedure. We're going to do some lip to lip *com*pressing. Okay? Head up please. *(She raises his head up.)* Good. Now, I want you to stay real still while I apply localized pressure.

(She goes in for the kiss. After a moment or two she pulls away and leaps off the couch in horror.)

WHO ARE YOU?!

TONY. What?!

ASHLEY. WHO THE HELL ARE YOU?!

TONY. That's what I've been trying to tell you.

ASHLEY. I mean, *(She grabs her glasses off the counter and puts them on.)* I mean, you may look like Prescott, in fact, you look a lot like Prescott, but, believe me, you are not Prescott! I want to know who in the Hell you are!

TONY. I can explain.

ASHLEY. What are you doing here pretending to be my husband? Who would do something like that? Are you hiding from someone? Are you a fugitive? You are, aren't you? *(She screams and pulls the gun out of her purse.)* You're that man who escaped from prison! Admit it!

TONY. *(starting to get up)* Now look I....

ASHLEY. *(pointing the gun at him)* I want you to stay right where you are! *(He moves a little.)* I'm not afraid to use this. I don't want to shoot you but I will if I have to. Now just stay real quiet while I step over here and call the police.

(She picks up the receiver and listens.)

Okay, there doesn't seem to be any dial tone. This phone seems to be dead. You wouldn't know anything about that, would you?

TONY. Maybe.

ASHLEY. I see. *(picking up the phone cord and seeing the cut end)* You cut the phone line. Well, let me tell you something, that isn't going to do you one bit of good because I have a cell phone right there in that purse.

(She points to the purse on the couch. TONY picks up the golf club and holds it over the purse.)

ASHLEY. What are you doing with that club?

TONY. Sorry.

(TONY smashes the club on the purse. There is a jaunty cell phone ring. TONY smashes it again. It dies.)

ASHLEY. Alright. You shouldn't have done that. That was a very bad thing to do. I don't know what you hope to accomplish with any of this. I am armed and somehow or other, even if I have to wait here for hours, you are going to end up back in police custody. My husband Prescott will be here very soon and when he arrives you are going to deeply regret causing all this trouble. The only thing I'm sorry about is Grandpa. He's been having some trouble with his heart and I don't want him to get all aggravated, so if you wouldn't mind, I'd like you to just sit there quietly while I try to figure this out.

TONY. You know, Ashley, I got some bad news for you.

ASHLEY. No, right now I'm afraid you're the one getting the bad news.

TONY. I mean it. What I've got to tell you is going to get you real unhappy.

ASHLEY. You can threaten all you want but it will not make things any better.

TONY. It's not that I want to make you unhappy. I just need to tell you who I am.

ASHLEY. Escaped murderer. We've got that.

TONY. Who I am and what I know.

ASHLEY. I'm really not interested.

TONY. Come on; aren't you even a little curious why I look so much like your husband?

ASHLEY. No. *(long pause)* All right, why do you?

(pause)

TONY. Did you know that horse's teeth have to be filed periodically?

ASHLEY. No.

TONY. Well they do. Or the teeth grow out funny and then they damage the horses' mouths. And it's a tough job. Filing them. You got to get jammed in a corral with the horse and hold on to its head and then the horse gets all spooked and frisky and tries to kick you and somehow in the middle of all that you got to pull out your file and get to work on the teeth.

ASHLEY. And this is going to explain why you look like Prescott?

TONY. Yes. See, that's what I used to do and it was a work-out but it was a job and lot of times it was outdoors and I'd get to travel and I love horses so it meant I got to work with them and work with their...teeth and one time I was hired by this little horse farm up in Georgia to help out with some over-bite palominos and after about a week of that I decided I needed to drive into town to get a drink and relax cause, you know, all that filing can make you pretty thirsty.

ASHLEY. I'll bet.

TONY. So I came in and had a couple beers in this little pool hall kind of tavern and I was just heading back to the horse farm when a cop pulled me over and arrested me.

ASHLEY. Good.

TONY. He arrested me for murder.

ASHLEY. Uh *huh*.

TONY. Seems some woman got stabbed to death in this walk-up apartment over by the pool hall and about half the town saw me with her before the murder and another big bunch saw me leaving her place after the murder, and one person who lived in a second story apartment across the street saw me committing the murder. But guess what?

ASHLEY. What?

TONY. I never saw that woman in my life.

ASHLEY. Everybody was wrong, huh?

TONY. Yup. They were all wrong.

ASHLEY. You know, I've heard that. I've heard that all the inmates in all the prisons say that they're innocent.

TONY. Ashley, I am innocent.

ASHLEY. See?

TONY. I really am.

ASHLEY. Even if you were innocent and I'm not saying you were or are or anything, but even if you were, what does any of this have to do with me?

TONY. All right now listen; about two months ago I was in the prison library. I'd been spending as much time as possible in there reading whatever I could get my hands on, going through things, working on my case; and one day I come across something that hit me like hoof in the stomach.

ASHLEY. What was that?

TONY. Your wedding announcement.

ASHLEY. Oh yeah? And why was that so…significant?

TONY. It wasn't the names or the date or the location or anything like that. It was the picture.

ASHLEY. What picture?

TONY. You and your husband. It was a real good picture.

ASHLEY. *(not meaning it)* I'm glad you liked it.

TONY. I could see your husband real clearly.

ASHLEY. Prescott.

TONY. Prescott. I just flat out could not believe the resemblance. I mean I've heard each of us has a double out there somewhere, but I never saw anything like this.

ASHLEY. I'm starting to think I know where you're going with this and I want you to know I think you're crazy.

TONY. That man looked exactly like me. Exactly.

ASHLEY. This is so silly.

TONY. Okay, I know. Not too much there really to work with. So we looked like each other. So what? But then I thought of something. Did you know you can check flight records over the phone?

ASHLEY. No.

TONY. You can. If you wanna know whether somebody flew on a certain day or if you wanna learn where someone flew to, you can pretend to be that person and if you call them and play it right, the airlines will look it up and tell you.

ASHLEY. So?

TONY. So guess who flew into Macon, Georgia on four different occasions around the time that Bonnie Mills was stabbed to death?

ASHLEY. You are really crazy.

TONY. Huh? Guess who?

ASHLEY. Prescott flies to all sorts of places all over the country. He is a busy, successful professional.

TONY. Ashley, you are married to a murderer.

ASHLEY. I can't believe I have to stand here and listen to this!

TONY. I'm telling you the truth.

ASHLEY. You are sick! You are a sick person! And you've got a helluva lot of nerve! Breaking into this house, deceiving an innocent old man, and then trying to implicate my husband in your disgusting, horrible crime. It's just beyond words. From now on, just don't say anything.

TONY. Okay.

ASHLEY. I mean it; I don't want to hear one peep out of you.

TONY. All right.

ASHLEY. Nothing.

(He nods.)

(a long pause)

You accidently see my husband's picture in the paper and from that you decide he's a murderer. I mean;

give me a break. (**TONY** *doesn't say anything.*) There are lots of people all over the world who look like each other but that doesn't mean they're murderers. That is absurd! And stupid! Did he fly in or out of Macon the day that woman was killed?

TONY. No, I can't prove he was in Macon on that day, but he visited Macon four times right before her death!

ASHLEY. See what I mean!? There's nothing there! I know my husband! All right? I know him! This woman was stabbed to death right?

TONY. Right.

ASHLEY. Prescott is not a stabber. That's ridiculous. He hates violence. You can cook up all the twisted fantasies you want, but you will never convince me, and you'll never convince anyone else either. No wonder you don't want me to call the police. Anyone in their right mind is going to just laugh themselves sick at this whole crazy theory.

TONY. That's why I needed to get here. To check it out myself. I called around. Called your husband's family. They told me where Prescott was going to be today. I needed to track this thing down.

ASHLEY. And how did you escape from prison?

TONY. Well let me just say this, the powers that be made a big mistake locking up a professional filer.

ASHLEY. What's your name?

TONY. Tony. Tony Rydell.

ASHLEY. Well, Tony Rydell you made a big mistake coming here. I can't believe the nerve of this whole thing.

TONY. I want to offer you a deal.

ASHLEY. No thanks. I'm not making any deals with you.

TONY. Listen to this; you're gonna like it.

ASHLEY. I'm not.

TONY. Here's the idea; let me hide somewhere around here and then when your husband arrives ask him just this one question.

ASHLEY. No way.

TONY. Ask him in 2009, where was he on the night of July 12th.

ASHLEY. I can tell you this; wherever he was, he was not murdering anybody.

TONY. Ask him.

ASHLEY. It's too stupid.

TONY. Ask him.

ASHLEY. First of all, I'm not going to take this gun off of you and let you go off and hide somewhere. Understand?

TONY. If he sees me, it's over. I need to be hidden. You want a real answer to the question you got to keep me out of the picture.

ASHLEY. *(sudden idea)* On the other hand, maybe we should tuck you away.

(She goes over to the closet and checks the lock. Pointing the gun, she goes up to **TONY.***)*

Alright; even though it's absolutely ridiculous I'll ask him. But you have to wait in that closet.

TONY. You're not gonna lock the door though right?

ASHLEY. I'm definitely gonna lock the door.

TONY. Then no deal. For one thing, after you say that date he'll freak out and you're going to need me.

ASHLEY. I won't need you because Prescott had nothing to do with the murder. But since I don't really want to be standing out here with a gun on you all afternoon *(gesturing to closet)* that's where I want you to go.

(waving the gun at him)

Stand up.

(He doesn't move.)

(pointing the gun more aggressively) I mean it! I really will shoot this.

(TONY *gets to his feet.)*

Now head over to the closet.

TONY. Ashley; this is a real bad idea.

ASHLEY. Keep moving. And no funny stuff.

(He is at the closet door.)

Okay, now step inside.

(TONY *steps inside the closet but backs out again to say:)*

TONY. You're making a big mistake.

(He goes in again and **ASHLEY** *is about to shut the door when [seemingly] a part of him [actually a double wearing Tony's clothes] is seen agressively backing out one more time.* **ASHLEY** *pushes her gun against this double and pushes him all the way in saying…)*

ASHLEY. All right. That's enough. Just calm down and get in there.

(She shuts and locks the door.)

(The little action with the double gives the actor playing **TONY** *time to change pants and get over to the front door. He bursts in carrying a large container.)*

PRESCOTT. *(with a flourish)* Hey Ashley, look who made it all the way from Savannah!

(curtain)

ACT TWO

(The action is continuous.)

ASHLEY. Prescott, at last you're here! Oh my God!

(They kiss.)

It really is you isn't it?

PRESCOTT. It's me alright.

ASHLEY. Thank God!

PRESCOTT. Another kiss. Ashley! At last! Lord, you look even more beautiful than I remembered.

ASHLEY. Thank you.

PRESCOTT. Absolutely radiant!

ASHLEY. We try.

PRESCOTT. Is it just me or does it seem like we've been apart forever?

ASHLEY. Oh Prescott, I think that was the longest three weeks anyone's ever had to endure.

PRESCOTT. An eternity –

(another kiss)

ASHLEY. Listen, right away I have to ask you this kind of crazy question.

PRESCOTT. Okay?

ASHLEY. *(noticing the large container)* …What is that?

PRESCOTT. This? Oh well I brought some iced tea with me for the drive.

ASHLEY. That's a lot of iced tea.

PRESCOTT. It's a long drive.

(He puts the container on the floor.)

ASHLEY. *(about to pick it up)* Shall I put it over in the kitchen.

PRESCOTT. *(stopping her)* You know what? It's not really
   drinkable any more. Somewhere en route it became
   luke warm tea.

ASHLEY. We could put ice cubes in it.

PRESCOTT. Too much trouble.

ASHLEY. I don't mind.

PRESCOTT. Really; don't bother. If we're gonna be fussing
   with ice cubes I'd rather we put them in something
   more...you know...alcoholic.

   (heading into the kitchen)

   You think Grandpa has anything to drink around here?

ASHLEY. I doubt it.

PRESCOTT. Oh that's right; dry Grandpa. Okay; orange
   juice! That's what I want. I'm in Florida and I want
   some Florida orange juice. *(He opens refrigerator.)*
   Alright, no orange juice. But he does have some
   oranges which I will magically transform into orange
   juice, using *(He takes the knife off the shelf with a flourish.)*
   only a simple carving knife.

   *(He puts the oranges on the table. As he brings over some
   glasses and a pitcher...)*

   Care to join me?

ASHLEY. No thanks. *(She looks back and forth from* **PRESCOTT**
   to the closet.) No, I just need to tell you something.

PRESCOTT. Oh yeah? What's going on?

ASHLEY. Well, it's kind of an amazing development. You
   know, as I said, I've really only been here about maybe
   a half an hour or so.

PRESCOTT. Right.

ASHLEY. But in that time something has occurred that's
   really pretty...well, that's kind of given me pause. In a
   way it's sort of insane, and I feel a little crazy that such
   an idea was even proposed to me.

PRESCOTT. I can't wait to hear.

ASHLEY. What's happened is that... *(She notices that* **PRESCOTT** *is inspecting the knife.)* this unexpected weirdness got going.

PRESCOTT. Between you and Grandpa.

ASHLEY. No you see, Grandpa isn't really aware of what's happened because I didn't want to get him all riled up.

PRESCOTT. So something occurred here that Grandpa doesn't yet know about. Is that it?

(He starts cutting.)

ASHLEY. Right.

PRESCOTT. Does this have something to do with the birth certificate?

ASHLEY. What?

PRESCOTT. The birth certificate you were supposed to ask Grandpa about. He does have it doesn't he?

ASHLEY. I don't know.

PRESCOTT. *(He stops cutting.)* You didn't ask him?!

ASHLEY. I asked him but we haven't had a chance to actually get it.

PRESCOTT. So what, you're...waiting for the moment?

ASHLEY. I guess.

PRESCOTT. Sweetheart, if Grandpa has the birth certificate getting it from him shouldn't be that complicated. Seems like a simple "Grandpa could I have your birth certificate" would do the job. Don't you think?

ASHLEY. I know but I really did just get here. We had to, you know, greet each other and then, as I was saying to you, this other thing happened. I mean why is it so important that you have the birth certificate instantly?

PRESCOTT. Okay that's fine; I don't need it. Forget I said I wanted to help with your family tree.

ASHLEY. Come on, don't get like that. I'm just asking why you have to have it the second you arrive.

PRESCOTT. *(back to cutting)* No I mean it. Let's change the subject.

ASHLEY. Prescott...

PRESCOTT. I thought it was going to be fun for us to explore your background together and learn about your roots and everything but if you're not into it, I say let's just skip the whole thing.

ASHLEY. Prescott I am into it. I love that you want to do this. I'll go ask him about it right now.

(*She turns to go, sees the closet, and turns back to* **PRESCOTT**. *The cutting is starting to look a little scary.*)

But first I want us to talk.

PRESCOTT. About what?

ASHLEY. This other issue.

PRESCOTT. Ashley I hate to say it but you know, you do this quite a bit.

ASHLEY. Do what?

PRESCOTT. This. This starting off on something and then turning around and shifting to something else.

ASHLEY. This isn't something else.

PRESCOTT. Oh, I'm sorry. I thought because you were going to go get the birth certificate and now you're changing the subject, that we had shifted to something else but what do I know? I'm just the guy who cuts the oranges.

ASHLEY. But what I need to talk to you about is important.

PRESCOTT. Okay, got it. (*taps head*) A little thick here sometimes but it's finally gotten through. You don't think the birth certificate is important.

ASHLEY. Yes I do.

PRESCOTT. Apparently not.

(*pause*)

ASHLEY. Would you like me to go get the birth certificate?

PRESCOTT. Noo! No! No! Oh my goodness!! Whatever gave you that idea?!

ASHLEY. Prescott sometimes you're very hard to talk to.

PRESCOTT. Me?! Hey, I'm not the one jumping from subject to subject and getting all bent out of..

ASHLEY. *(yelling)* PRESCOTT!

PRESCOTT. What?

ASHLEY. LISTEN TO ME!!

> *(trying to collect herself)*

> Look, I want you to know I have absolutely no belief that there's even a particle of a chance that anything that was said has any validity whatso...

> **(PRESCOTT**'s *knife cutting suddenly looks to* **ASHLEY** *a little vicious.)*

> ...Alright, I have a question for you.

PRESCOTT. Okay?

ASHLEY. Where were you on the night of...

> *(She pauses.)*

PRESCOTT. On the night of what? What are you talking about?

ASHLEY. It's just this thing I wanted to ask you about.

PRESCOTT. What thing?

> *(pause)*

ASHLEY. Alright let me put it all another way; when you do your genealogy, you're having to deal with dead people right?

PRESCOTT. *(back to working on the juice)* Not directly. I've found that when I'm conducting a genealogical investigation, dead people don't have too much to say for themselves.

ASHLEY. So dead people aren't really relevant. To you.

PRESCOTT. What's all this about?

ASHLEY. I guess I'm just kind of curious.

PRESCOTT. I wish I could tell better what the topic of this conversation is. It sounds interesting.

ASHLEY. It's just that there's this question, this kind of strange question I want to ask and when I explain why I'm asking it you're going to be pretty amazed. But what I need to let you know is, I'm not asking because I'm suspicious or anything. It's just something I need to find out about to clear the air.

PRESCOTT. I get it. *(affectionately)* Sweetheart. That's so cute. You little worry-wart. Okay, I'm going to make you feel much better. I'm going to assure you of something that's going to put your mind completely at rest. Ashley, I want you to know that I have been absolutely faithful to you throughout our whole marriage. That's right. I have been true to you during the entire three weeks.

ASHLEY. Well, that is good to know but...

PRESCOTT. It hasn't been easy but I toed the line and hung in there. You sure you don't want any of this?

ASHLEY. No thanks.

PRESCOTT. That's right sweetheart; true blue. Absolute fidelity. You have got yourself a loyal husband and anyone who says different had better be careful because *(holding juice in one hand and knife in the other)* I am orange cutter.

(He takes a swig of the juice.)

ASHLEY. *(blurting it out while he's drinking)* In 2009, where were you on the night of July twelfth?

(Choking on his drink, he has a coughing fit and is spitting out juice.)

PRESCOTT. *(between coughs)* Just a second.

(He rushes into the bathroom.)

(She rushes over to the closet door and in a stage whisper says..)

ASHLEY. What do I do? He's in the bathroom.

TONY. *(through the closet door)* Lock the bathroom door.

ASHLEY. I can't.

TONY. Do it!

(She rushes up to the bathroom door and slams it shut. Then she locks it.)

PRESCOTT. *(from inside)* Hey! Why'd you shut the door?! *(pounding)* Open this door. Ashley! Ashley are you out there?! *(more pounding)*

ASHLEY. The door is locked.

PRESCOTT. Well, unlock it.

ASHLEY. I can't.

PRESCOTT. Just turn the knob thing.

ASHLEY. Um...It doesn't seem to work. I better go find Grandpa.

(She rushes up to the closet.)

Now what do I do?

TONY. Let me out!

ASHLEY. No. I can't.

TONY. Do it!

ASHLEY. No! I don't trust you either.

(She lets out a stifled scream and rushes out the back door. GRANDPA enters through the front door and hears pounding coming from inside the bathroom. He points to it and says..)

Bathroom.

(He goes up to the door and opens it.)

Well, what happened to you?

PRESCOTT. To me? The door got locked. But wait! Hold it! Don't tell me, let me guess; you're Mr. Deemer. Am I right?

GRANDPA. Yes, but as I said before, you can call me Grandpa.

PRESCOTT. *(emotionally)* Grandpa!! *(big hug)* I can't tell you how happy I am to meet you. I've heard so much about you. Grandpa!! *(another hug)* Well, you're just as Ashley described you. Except she didn't tell me you were so young!

GRANDPA. You're going to have to speak up a bit. My hearing's a little off and on today.

PRESCOTT. I'm saying you look so young.

GRANDPA. Who does?

PRESCOTT. You do.

GRANDPA. I do what?

PRESCOTT. Look young.

GRANDPA. What?

PRESCOTT. LOOK YOUNG.

GRANDPA. What?

PRESCOTT. LOOK YOUNG!!

GRANDPA. I'd like to, but it's hard when you're born during the Hoover administration.

(awkward pause)

PRESCOTT. Grandpa! *(another hug)*

GRANDPA. Yes, well it's nice to have you here and I certainly hope you'll make yourself at home and just feel free to do whatever you want like, I don't know, play golf. Do you ever play golf?

PRESCOTT. Oh yes, I love golf.

GRANDPA. You do?!

PRESCOTT. Sure, it's a passion of mine.

GRANDPA. Well, why didn't you say so? Want to play a round now?

PRESCOTT. Now? No, right now wouldn't be good. But possibly later?

GRANDPA. Don't be so sure about later. Time marches on you know. I don't want to alarm you, but let's face it; in the near future one of us might suddenly have a heart attack and drop dead and then who will I play with.

PRESCOTT. Grandpa, sorry, I can't play now. I need to ask you about something and then I need to go find my wife.

GRANDPA. Oh yes, your wife, Ashley. Little Ashley. I wanted to say to you, by the way, that I was so sorry that I couldn't get to your wedding.

PRESCOTT. No, I completely understand. Now Grandpa, I'm hoping your birth certificate is som....

GRANDPA. Ashley being my only living relative and all and given how much I love her it just about broke my heart not to be there, but sometimes circumstances prevent you from doing what you most want to do.

PRESCOTT. Of course they do. I'm wondering if your Birth Cer...

GRANDPA. Cause as it happens the club here has only twelve Senior Tournaments a year.

(a beat)

PRESCOTT. Grandpa, do you still have your birth certificate?

GRANDPA. Well, yes. Pretty sure I do. Somewhere. I know it's around here because every now and then at the senior tournaments they card you.

PRESCOTT. If you don't mind then do me a favor and find it while I go out and look for Ashley. Alright?

GRANDPA. You bet.

(**PRESCOTT** *exits out the front door.* **GRANDPA** *heads towards the closet. Pointing at the door.)*

Closet

(He's almost at the closet when **ASHLEY** *enters through the back door. Seeing* **GRANDPA** *about to open the closet door...)*

ASHLEY. Grandpa!

GRANDPA. What?

ASHLEY. Grandpa, don't open that door!

GRANDPA. Why?

ASHLEY. Cause I want you to get back to work on the garden...While there's still light.

GRANDPA. You do?

ASHLEY. *(leading him away from the closet)* Yes, I've got a few things to take care of in here with Prescott. If you don't mind.

GRANDPA. *(shaking his head and laughing as he starts heading out)* I know; you little lovebir…

(noticing Prescott's container on the floor)

What's this?

ASHLEY. Oh, Prescott brought some ice tea with him.

GRANDPA. Ice tea, huh? Don't mind if I do.

(He picks it up and moves towards the kitchen.)

*(Wanting to get **GRANDPA** outside, she grabs a glass off the table and heads him back towards the back door. Handing him the glass.)*

ASHLEY. Good idea; you can have a nice glass of ice tea out in the garden.

(GRANDPA's almost out the door.)*

He did say though it's gotten a little warm.

GRANDPA. *(As he exits, sticking his head outside and looking around to test the temperature.)* He's got a point.

(exit)

ASHLEY. *(rushing over to the bathroom door and listening and then dashing over to the close)* Tony?

TONY. Ashley, you got to open this door!

ASHLEY. I don't think I can do that! I can't be turning you loose just based on this crazy idea you told me which I have no way of knowing whether or not is even remotely….

PRESCOTT. *(coming in through the front door)* Ashley!! *(She freezes.)* There you are. I've been looking for you.

ASHLEY. Prescott! How did you get out of the bathroom?

PRESCOTT. Grandpa.

ASHLEY. Grandpa? Oh. Good. I was thinking he'd be able to "get you out." In fact, that's where I was; off looking for him. Now it turns out he got in here ahead of me.

(a strained laugh)

PRESCOTT. Come here, you.

ASHLEY. What?

PRESCOTT. Come over here.

ASHLEY. There?

PRESCOTT. Here. Come on.

ASHLEY. Um…why?

PRESCOTT. *(baby-talk)* Hubby want hug.

ASHLEY. Oh, okay.

(She goes up to him and they hug.)

PRESCOTT. *(wrapped around* **ASHLEY***)* This is nice isn't it?

ASHLEY. Oh yeah.

PRESCOTT. You can't ask for much more than this.

ASHLEY. No. You can't.

PRESCOTT. Grandpa's great.

ASHLEY. Isn't he?

PRESCOTT. Just a wonderful wonderful old fellow. And this house is cute.

ASHLEY. Isn't it?

PRESCOTT. It's a cute house.

ASHLEY. Cute house. Cute house. No question about it. This house is absolutely cu…

PRESCOTT. Ashley?

ASHLEY. Yes?

PRESCOTT. Did you lock me in the bathroom?

ASHLEY. What do you mean?

PRESCOTT. I mean, I went in there and it seemed as though you slammed the door shut and locked it.

ASHLEY. *(breaking out of hug)* No. Not at all. I didn't do that. Why would I do that?

PRESCOTT. I don't know. Somehow that door did get shut though right?

ASHLEY. I think the wind must have blown it.

PRESCOTT. The wind.

ASHLEY. Yeah.

PRESCOTT. That's funny, I haven't really noticed a lot of wind blowing through here. I didn't realize we were in a high wind velocity locale.

(shrugging) Hmmph. It's too bad the ceiling isn't higher or we could have some fun in here with kites.

ASHLEY. Or maybe the door just shuts automatically.

PRESCOTT. That's probably it, it's one of those automatic shut-the-bathroom-door-automatically devices you hear so much about. I'd like to go take a look at that.

(He goes over and steps partly inside the bathroom and starts fooling with the door.)

Well, that's odd; I can't seem to find any door shutting mechanism here. None at all. I guess we're back to the wind theory. Let's see how that might work.

(stepping all the way in) Now I'll stand in here and let's wait and see if a big gust comes along. *(pause)* Nothing so far. *(pause)* Anything out there? Any little breeze starting up? *(pause)* Any...

*(**ASHLEY** rushes up to the door and slams it and locks it. Emotionally exhausted, she leans against the door and pants.)*

(from inside) Ashley, open this door! Open it! Are you out there? I know it was you that shut it. Now come on now, open up. I mean it. Right this second. You hear me!?

(pause)

ASHLEY. I can't open the door.

PRESCOTT. Why not.

ASHLEY. I just can't.

PRESCOTT. Yes, you can. Unlock it and turn the knob.

ASHLEY. *(Going over to the closet. Now speaking quietly.)* Are you in there?

TONY. *(from inside)* Yes.

ASHLEY. What do I do?

PRESCOTT. *(pounding)*

TONY. Don't open that door.

(*more pounding from* **PRESCOTT**)

ASHLEY. But I can't just keep him locked in the bathroom.

TONY. Yes, you can.

ASHLEY. (*more pounding*) He's my husband.

TONY. Listen, he's a murderer. You must not let him out. You've got to let me out! Do you understand. Not him. Me. Don't open that door.

ASHLEY. Why should I listen to you? You're an escaped convict.

(*pounding from* **PRESCOTT**)

TONY. Trust me.

(*more pounding*)

ASHLEY. No, I'm not going to have everything completely torn apart because of a strange man who I've never met in my life before, who himself may very well be a murderer but even if he's not a murderer, he's someone who told me that what he does for a living is file horses' teeth!

(*Unseen by* **ASHLEY**, **PRESCOTT** *enters through the back door and quietly walks up to her as she's talking.*)

I won't let everything I've been dreaming of all my life be destroyed by a horse tooth fi...

PRESCOTT. (*suddenly*) Ashley?

(**ASHLEY** *jumps in the air.*)

ASHLEY. Ahhh!

(*gasping for air and clutching her chest*)

Prescott!! Oh my God. What a fright! Oh you just scared the sh...living daylights out of me. Lord! How did you get out of the bathroom?

PRESCOTT. Window. This time I used the window. Even though it was a little undignified I decided that crawling out the window would get me out of the bathroom sooner than waiting for you.

ASHLEY. I was going to open the door.

PRESCOTT. I'm glad to hear that. But you see the problem was in the meantime I was getting a little tired of the bathroom. After a while I felt as if I had more or less done the bathroom. Hence the bathroom window. Now Ashley, I have a question for you.

ASHLEY. Okay.

PRESCOTT. Who were you talking to?

ASHLEY. When?

PRESCOTT. Just now.

ASHLEY. You mean over there?

PRESCOTT. Yes, over there by the closet. I'm wondering if somebody is in the closet?

(pause)

ASHLEY. Maybe.

PRESCOTT. Who?

ASHLEY. A man.

PRESCOTT. What man?

ASHLEY. A man who said some things.

PRESCOTT. Said some things about what?

ASHLEY. About you.

PRESCOTT. Okay, what kind of things?

ASHLEY. Bad things.

PRESCOTT. So let me get this straight; there's a man in the closet – locked in the closet?

ASHLEY. Yes.

PRESCOTT. There's a man locked in the closet who has been saying some bad things about me. Is that the situation?

ASHLEY. That's right.

PRESCOTT. And let me guess; the bad things he said made you want to lock me in the bathroom. Is that it?

ASHLEY. Yes. But I was going to let you out because I've realized I don't really trust the man in the closet.

PRESCOTT. Okay. Good. Then if it wouldn't be too much trouble, I think this might be a good moment – right now – for you to tell me; who is the man in the closet?

ASHLEY. It's that convict. The prisoner who escaped.

PRESCOTT. *(floored)* What?!

ASHLEY. The escapee. You need to know though that...

PRESCOTT. The one they've been looking for? The one on the news? Jesus! And he's in that closet right there?

ASHLEY. Yes.

PRESCOTT. *(shocked)* Whoa! Amazing! Right behind that door?

(starts pacing)

ASHLEY. *(She nods.)* And before he went in there he told me all these crazy ideas that I ....

PRESCOTT. Like what?

ASHLEY. Like he said..

PRESCOTT. I can't believe he's in there.

ASHLEY. ...like he said that – and you've got to understand I do not believe him – at all – he said that...it was you who killed the woman.

PRESCOTT. What woman?

ASHLEY. The woman in Macon, Georgia.

PRESCOTT. Back up; there was a woman killed in Macon, Georgia?

ASHLEY. Yes and he was convicted of killing her.

PRESCOTT. Go on.

ASHLEY. But he said that while he was in the prison library after getting sentenced he decided that you did it and...

PRESCOTT. Killed the woman.

ASHLEY. *(rapidly)* Yes; killed the woman, and on the phone he was able to check your flight records and he found out you had flown in and out of Macon a bunch of times.

(a beat)

PRESCOTT. Okay, Ashley, first of all – and you need to know I'm telling the absolute truth here – in my whole life I have never flown in or out of Macon, Georgia. Okay? Not once. So we can eliminate that part of the concept right off the bat.

ASHLEY. But what about the flight records?

PRESCOTT. One person cannot access another person's flight records. Airlines have built big security walls to prevent that. Passwords. Codes. You can't break through. So saying he checked my flight records is ridiculous.

ASHLEY. But it's not just that. He also said he was singled out as the killer because he looked exactly like the real killer who according to him was....basically....you.

PRESCOTT. Now we're beyond ridiculous.

ASHLEY. But Prescott, at first, when I first saw him, I honestly had trouble telling you two apart. That's what threw me; the idea that this man could be in this house – a house you were today coming to visit – and turn out to look just like you.

PRESCOTT. You know what? I admit it; that is weird but.... Okay; how did he get into the house?

ASHLEY. I don't know. I think maybe while Grandpa was out he snuck in.

PRESCOTT. Who found him?

ASHLEY. Grandpa. And see? Grandpa thought he was you as well. But later when I talked to him *(gestures to closet)* alone he told me who he was and said he came here hunting around for you.

PRESCOTT. Hmm...I've got to admit; it *is* hard to explain why apparently – and I'm taking you're word for it here – why apparently he looks so much like me.

ASHLEY. That's the big puzzle.

PRESCOTT. So in a way I don't blame you for getting a little confu... *(big idea)* Wait a second! Hold everything.

ASHLEY. What?

PRESCOTT. That's it! I know what happened. I know exactly what happened.

ASHLEY. You do? What?

PRESCOTT. Prisoner on the loose. Manhunt. Dogs. Helicopters. He's crashing around the woods out there and suddenly he comes across this little clearing and spots the house, and while Grandpa is out in the garden or playing golf or something he breaks in. Alright?

ASHLEY. Okay...

PRESCOTT. So he's in here, he's looking at things poking around and all of a sudden – bingo – he spots...this wedding announcement.

(tapping the announcement)

Right here. And when he sees how much we look alike he cooks up the crazy me-flying-into-Macon-Georgia scenario. See? I'll bet anything that's what happened. All this nonsense about me being a killer came directly from him spotting this wedding photo. That's got to be it. Right?

ASHLEY. *(half heartedly)* Right.

PRESCOTT. Could you punch that up a little?

ASHLEY. *(more conviction)* Right!

(pause)

PRESCOTT. Okay what else?

ASHLEY. He told me to ask you what you were doing on the night of July 12th, and when I did, you had a coughing fit with your juice. I think that was what threw me the most. The coughing.

PRESCOTT. *(laughing affectionately)* Oh, sweetheart. Oh my goodness. I just happened to get some juice caught in my throat. It was pulpy. It went down wrong. I mean that's pretty wild; I choke on a little pulp and suddenly I'm a murderer.

ASHLEY. I'm sorry.

PRESCOTT. No. I mean I'm sorry. I'm sorry I haven't been enough of a presence in your life that you don't know I would never harm a living soul.

ASHLEY. I guess I just – cause of the choking and the other things he said – got kind of confused.

(She starts to cry. **PRESCOTT** *puts her head against his shoulder.)*

PRESCOTT. Now listen you little impressionable angel, we're gonna put all this behind us. Alright?

ASHLEY. *(emotionally)* Yes. All right. Thanks.

(More hugging. Finally:)

Prescott, do you have your cell phone with you?

PRESCOTT. *(patting his pocket)* Yeah?

ASHLEY. Well then, don't you think we should call the police?

PRESCOTT. Definitely. That's just what I'm going to do. But I want to make sure that everything's secure first, okay? Closet locked up tight and all that. And I really need to get you out of harm's way. I want you to go out to the garden and find Grandpa and I want both of you to stay out there – as far away as possible – till I say it's safe to come in. Okay?

ASHLEY. *(starting to go)* Okay.

PRESCOTT. Hey wait, do you know if Grandpa has any duct tape?

ASHLEY. There might be some in the hardware drawer next to the sink.

PRESCOTT. Okay. And how about a vacuum cleaner?

ASHLEY. I think there's one in the cabinet by the refrigerator? But why in the world do you need a vacuum cleaner?

PRESCOTT. I don't need it. It's just to help me get oriented. You know; unfamiliar house – where are the appliances?

ASHLEY. Oh.

PRESCOTT. So off you go and I'll take care of everything in here.

ASHLEY. Okay. And Prescott, I just want you to know how awful I feel abou....

(She starts to head out the back door.)

PRESCOTT. Hey, let's not have any more of that. Everybody makes mistakes. That's why they put erasers on pencils. That's why they have a delete button. So come on, sweetheart; you better get going.

(ASHLEY starts to leave but turns at the door. They blow each other kisses.)

(Night is falling and the stage is slowly darkening)

(Once he's sure Ashley's gone, PRESCOTT tears into the kitchen, opens the drawer, grabs the duct tape, pulls open the cabinet door and grabs the vacuum cleaner. Carrying these, he rushes back into the living room and puts the vacuum cleaner on the table. He then disconnects the hose and pulls off the wide mouth attachment replacing it with the narrow-nozzle attachment, after which he puts the vacuum cleaner on the floor and carries the hose and the duct tape over to the oven. With the tape he attaches the open end of the hose to the gas outlet on the stove, and puts the nozzle end at the base of the closet door taping it into place so that it opens into the door crack. He grabs a kitchen towel from the sink and pushes it into the crack along the floor. Then he turns on the gas, pausing to listen to the hiss.)

(After double-checking his work, he heads towards the back door and exits.)

(The room is empty. All that is heard is the hiss of the gas. After a moment there's a pounding noise coming from inside the closet door. It builds into an explosion of fist-drumming and then starts quieting down. After a few weak final pounds, it stops.)

(There is knocking at the front door.)

MURIEL. *(O.S.)* Hello? Hello-o? Anybody home? *(Knock knock)* Hello?

(She enters through the front door leaving it open.)

Anyone here? Mr. Deemer? It's Muriel Carlan. *(semi-laugh)* Again.

(She comes farther into the room and looks around.)

Mr. Deemer? I'm afraid I'm barging in once more. Yoo hoo. Is anyone here? I wanted to....

(She notices the gas rig.)

Hmmm...

(Puzzled she hesitantly walks over to the oven. She looks at where the hose attaches to the stove and follows it down to where it outlets at the base of the closet. Going back to the oven she cocks her head down, sniffs a little, and listens to the escaping gas. Suddenly horrified but not sure what to do, she starts backing away towards the front door. As she nears it she quietly turns around and is about to exit when – with terrifying intensity— **PRESCOTT** *bursts through the door.)*

PRESCOTT. *(as he bursts)* Ah hah!

MURIEL. *(Frozen. Horrified. Gasping.)*

PRESCOTT. So there you are! At last. I've been waiting and waiting, trying to deal with the situation but it's not really my area of expertise.

MURIEL. *(more gasping)* I...I..

PRESCOTT. When I looked through the window and saw you checking out the rig over there I had to rush in .
and assure you that...

(He notices that **MURIEL** *is still trying to catch her breath.)*

I'm sorry. Did I startle you?

(Too frazzled to talk, she nods.)

You see I wanted you to understand right away it was just an improvised stop-gap kind of thing.

MURIEL. *(gasp gasp)* What was?

PRESCOTT. *(pointing to the closet, taking her arm, leading her over)* This. Over here. I'm sure someone with your experience could whip together a much more effective set-up but hey that's why you're the professional. I've got to admit though – I frankly wasn't expecting them to send a woman.

MURIEL. Who?

PRESCOTT. Who? Whoever I talked to. I thought they'd send a man. Isn't that terrible? All the progress women have made and I'm still assuming there's a pest control glass ceiling.

MURIEL. Pest control.

PRESCOTT. And now that you've come all the way out here, it may be that I've already solved the problem.

MURIEL. What problem?

PRESCOTT. Raccoon.

MURIEL. Raccoon?

PRESCOTT. Yes. As I explained on the phone; raccoon infestation. Actually I hope it's just one – one raccoon – so maybe infestation isn't the word. What do you think? Can one raccoon infest?

MURIEL. I wouldn't know.

PRESCOTT. But whatever; one is plenty. After he got cornered here in the closet, I rigged up my little gas line and turned it on. And from the sound of things I very well might have solved the problem.

MURIEL. The raccoon problem.

PRESCOTT. Right.

MURIEL. I'm afraid that somehow you've confused me with an exterminator.

PRESCOTT. *(seemingly shocked)* You mean you're not an exterminator?

MURIEL. No. No, I'm not.

PRESCOTT. Oh my goodness. I'm so embarrassed.

MURIEL. *(Trying to appear calm. Trying to politely break free and head for the door.)* No. Don't be. Easy mistake to make. And now if you'll excuse me I'll just be on my way...

PRESCOTT. *(not releasing her)* Wait. You just got here.

MURIEL. Yes, but since you're busy...

PRESCOTT. I'm not though. I was. Now I just need to confirm that my devise worked and then I'm all done.

MURIEL. I do actually have to be running along.

PRESCOTT. Aren't you curious to see if my little gizmo accomplished the mission?

MURIEL. I actually really don't want to see a dead raccoon.

PRESCOTT. Maybe he's not dead.

MURIEL. Either way.

PRESCOTT. Just one little peek and then you can get going.

MURIEL. I'd like to get going without the little peek. And frankly I'd like you to let go of my arm.

PRESCOTT. Tiny little peek.

MURIEL. No. I'm serious.

PRESCOTT. Teeny. Teeny. Teeny little peek.

MURIEL. No.

PRESCOTT. Teensy weensy peens....

(**MURIAL** *breaks free of his grip and makes a dash for the door but is tackled by* **PRESCOTT** *just behind the couch. While she is on the floor, hidden from view,* **PRESCOTT** *grabs a golf club, raises it over his head and deliveries a vicious blow. He then drags her limp body over to the closet, cautiously unlocks the door, opens it, and pushes* **MURIEL** *inside. He shuts the door, re-locks it, pushes the hose and towels back into place Then rushes out the back door.)*

(**GRANDPA** *enters through the front door and walks to the middle of the room. Pausing while he tries to remember why he'd come in. Suddenly pointing at the bathroom door.)*

GRANDPA. Bathroom.

(He goes into bathroom and shuts the door.)

(There is a muffled thumping noise followed by the sound of the inside door-trim cracking as it's being pried off. Muriel's colorful file is then seen pushing through the crack above the knob. The file descends and begins loudly working through the bolt. After a frenzy of aggressive sawing, there is a click and the door bursts open.)

*(**TONY**, gasping, holding a cloth over his face with one hand and Muriel's nail file in the other, somehow manages to drag a collapsed **MURIEL** toward the couch. He lays her down on it, then rushes back to the closet and pushes towel and hose back into position. Then he hurries back to **MURIEL** and starts to give her mouth to mouth resuscitation.)*

*(**GRANDPA** at this point, unseen by **TONY** and **MURIEL**, enters from the bathroom and is horrified by what he thinks is furtive passion.)*

(Stepping away from the bathroom door he hovers in the stairwell where he's not so noticeable.)

*(As **MURIEL** comes to...)*

TONY. Come on! Come on!

MURIEL. What's happening? What is it? Something exploded. *(groan)* I can't think.

TONY. You got nailed.

MURIEL. *(groan)* Oh God! I'm so weak. *(groan)* How did we get here?

TONY. When you landed on top of me I came to.

MURIEL. You came too?

TONY. *(showing **MURIEL** the file)* Yeah, and after some groping around in there, I got this, pushed it through the opening and gave it everything I had.

MURIEL. *(groans)*

TONY. But we can't stay on this couch. We don't want to get caught. Let's go. We've got to get into the bathroom.

(Getting his arm under her, he lifts her up and together they make it into the bathroom.)

GRANDPA. *(Shocked by what he has just witnessed, he heads for the back door. Calling out:)* Ashley. Ashley honey, we need to have a little talk. 'Fraid I got some bad news.

(He exits.)

(Just as the back door closes, a traumatized and gagging **ASHLEY** *bursts through the front door carrying the revolver in one hand and an empty glass in the other. In a stage whisper as she heads to the closet;)*

ASHLEY. Tony. *(gag)* You were right the whole time. *(gag gag)* Prescott's been lying. That stuff he brought with him? *(gag) THAT WAS NOT ICED TEA! (gag)* I'm so sorry I...

(She notices the gas rig.)

Oh my God! Tony!

(She turns off the gas then puts the gun and the glass on the table so she can dismantle the rig.)

Please be okay!

(She yanks away the vacuum cleaner hose, pulls the door open, and discovers the closet is empty.)

(Looking around. Stage whisper.)

Tony?

PRESCOTT. *(offstage)* Ashley. Where'd you go?

(Terrified, **ASHLEY** *looks around trying to figure out what to do.)*

(offstage) Ashley!

(For lack of any better idea **ASHLEY** *races to the stairwell and heads upstairs.)*

(entering through the front door) Hey sweetheart, where are you?

(He looks around. Calling out:)

Ashley!

(a pause)

Ashley? Did you....

(He spots the open door to the closet and rushes over to it. Seeing that Tony and Muriel are gone, he spins around frantically trying to figure out what happened. He sees the gun on the table, rushes over and grabs it, holding it up then instantly putting it behind his back so it can't be seen.)

(A thump from upstairs.)

(**PRESCOTT** *cocks his ear and listens.)*

(Another thump.)

(Cautiously, he heads over to the stairwell. He looks up the stairs trying to decide whether he dare go up there. Suddenly he spots the megaphone on the floor and has an idea.)

(He rushes over, picks it up, and tears out the front door.)

(**GRANDPA** *enters from the back door.)*

GRANDPA. Ashley? Ashley, I need to tell you something.

(A quick look towards the bathroom. Whispering.)

I got some news about your husband.

(Not seeing Ashley he turns and goes back out the back door.)

Ashley….

PRESCOTT. *(Southern cop voice. Coming from the direction of the front door. Through the megaphone.)* ATTENTION EVERYONE; THIS IS THE POLICE. REPEAT; THIS IS THE POLICE.

(The bathroom door pops open and **MURIEL,** *still woozy from the head smash, sticks her head out.)*

BE ADVISED THAT THIS HOUSE IS NOW SURROUNDED AND EVERYBODY INSIDE NEEDS TO COME OUT RIGHT NOW – HANDS OVER THEIR HEADS.

(Groggily, holding her head, **MURIEL** *staggers further into the room.)*

AGAIN; THE POLICE HAVE SURROUNDED THE
HOUSE AND YOU ALL NEED TO COME OUT THE
FRONT DOOR RIGHT NOW WITH YOUR HANDS
UP.

(The following should be lightening fast.)

TONY. *(Leaning in from the bathroom. Whispering intensely to* **MURIEL**.*)* What are you doing? Get back here.

MURIEL. It's the police. I need to tell them who the real killer is.

TONY. *(Still shaky from the gas, he stumbles towards* **MURIEL**.*)* Wait! That's not the police!

PRESCOTT. THIS IS THE POLICE…

TONY. *(gesturing)* Get down!

MURIEL. It's time they knew exactly what's going on.

TONY. *(Trying to catch up. Gesturing for* **MURIEL** *to crouch.)* You're too exposed!

MURIEL. I need to straighten them out.

TONY. *(grabbing her and trying to pull her lower)* Down! We got to stay outta sight! It's a trap!

PRESCOTT. …AND THIS IS YOUR FINAL WARNING.

MURIEL. *(Breaking free. Calling out.)* I'm coming!

PRESCOTT. YOU HAVE EXACTLY ONE MINUTE.

MURIEL. *(calling out)* Just a second.

TONY. It's cause you got smashed in the head.

PRESCOTT. STEP OUT THE DOOR RIGHT NOW.

MURIEL. *(Breaking loose again and making it to the front door. Calling out.)* Hold you're fire, I'm comi…

(Determined to stop her and keep her out of sight, **TONY** *grabs her to pull her lower – an act which sends both of them crashing to the floor.)*

GRANDPA. *(Entering from the back door. Seeing* **TONY** *and* **MURIEL** *entwined on the floor. Pointing and calling out:)* You two got to cut that out!

ASHLEY. *(entering from the stairs)* Tony!

TONY. *(Still crouching he gets to his feet.)* Ashley!

MURIEL. *(also rising)* Ashley?

TONY. *(while he holds down* **MURIEL.** *To* **ASHLEY)** Ashley where's that gun?

GRANDPA. What gun?

ASHLEY. He's got it.

GRANDPA. Who?

TONY. *(to* **MURIEL)** Listen; that's not the police. That's Prescott out there. He's armed.

MURIEL. Prescott.

TONY. And I really don't like these sightlines. Too many windows. Everybody get way down.

(MURIEL and ASHLEY drop to their knees.)

GRANDPA. What?

TONY. Get down!

GRANDPA. Why?

ASHLEY. It's complicated. We just better be on the floor.

GRANDPA. If you say so.

(GRANDPA gets on his knees)

TONY. I'm going to check these windows. Wanna make sure they're locked.

(He rushes over to the stage right window and pulls it shut, then starts checking the other ones.)

GRANDPA. Did somebody lose something?

ASHLEY. No, Grandpa.

MURIEL. *(fully recovered)* I'll check the window in the bathroom.

(She crouch-walks into the bathroom)

ASHLEY. *(to* TONY*)* Who is she?!

GRANDPA. I believe her name is Murel. She was…Good Lord; I can't believe it!

ASHLEY & TONY. What?!

GRANDPA. *(reaching under the couch)* The T.V. remote!

MURIEL. *(Coming out. To* **TONY***)* It's locked now. He can't get in that way.

GRANDPA. What way?

TONY. Yeah we got to keep him out.

ASHLEY. He is sick. He's totally sick! There's no question this is the evilist thing that ever was! *(She screams in frustration.)*

(pause)

GRANDPA. I feel like I'm missing something.

ASHLEY. Oh my God! Grandpa! Listen Grandpa, try not to get all upset but...but...SAND TRAP!!

GRANDPA. Oh dear!

ASHLEY. It's definitely sand trap time. I got to tell you something. Something terrible. I don't think I can keep it from you any longer.

GRANDPA. What is it?

ASHLEY. I am married to a murderer.

GRANDPA. *(angrily shaking his finger at* **TONY***)* All right, now you've gone too far!

PRESCOTT. *(from outside, using the megaphone)* Hey listen everybody, I want us to try and settle this in a mature, responsible way.

GRANDPA. That's my megaphone.

ASHLEY. Shhh...

PRESCOTT. Believe me, I don't want to cause any trouble. Whatever you're all thinking in there, you need to know that I'm not a dangerous murderer or anything like that. As it happens I am a simple genealogist who needs a certain birth certificate. That's all. What I'd like you to do now is slip the birth certificate under the front door. We don't need any confrontations. Okay? Under the door. Not a big deal.

GRANDPA. Who is that?

ASHLEY. That's Prescott.

GRANDPA. *(pointing at* **TONY***)* Well, then who is that?

ASHLEY. That's an escaped convict.

GRANDPA. You don't say.

ASHLEY. Listen Grandpa, the man I married turns out to be horrible. Just a monster. *(She starts choking up.)* He murders people and gets other people convicted instead of him and now he's trying to murder us!

*(**GRANDPA** takes her in his arms.)*

GRANDPA. There there. Come on, it's not so bad.

ASHLEY. How can you say it's not so bad.

GRANDPA. Well…now I'm not sorry I missed the wedding.

ASHLEY. Why is Prescott wanting to kill everybody? Why? He has a successful career and we have or at least had a nice future with so many things including a beautiful complete set of flatware. Why would he want to mess all that up? It's not like people just become murderers for no reason.

MURIEL. Oh, he had a reason all right.

ASHLEY. What?

MURIEL. Money.

ASHLEY. Come on, I don't have any money and neither does Grandpa.

TONY. *(From the window. Peering out.)* I can't figure out where he is.

ASHLEY. So how does money come into it?

MURIEL. Lakewood Rushton. Ever heard of him?

ASHLEY. The millionaire?

MURIEL. The billionaire. *(rapidly)* Lakewood Rushton didn't have any relatives. No kin. This bothered Lakewood Rushton because he had everything else. So he hired me to see if I could dig up any relations. I sent out word to county record offices all over the country, and one of them actually found something. Bonnie Mills, a records officer in Macon County Georgia, uncovered a link between Rushton, you, and your grandfather. You two turn out to be the only living relatives of Lakewood Rushton.

ASHLEY. Really!

MURIEL. But Bonnie Mills made a big mistake. She needed help with documentation, and instead of contacting me right away she looked up a professional genealogist.

ASHLEY. Prescott!

MURIEL. Right she hired Prescott. And when he arrived and learned how much money was at stake, he decided he wanted in on it.

ASHLEY. By marrying me!

MURIEL. Yes, but he needed Bonnie Mills to keep quiet.

ASHLEY. Oh my God!

MURIEL. At first he couldn't do anything drastic because they'd been seen together in Macon. But once he spotted Tony...

TONY. My lucky day.

MURIEL. ...he became homicidal.

ASHLEY. He killed her!

MURIEL. Yes.

GRANDPA. That *is* homicidal.

ASHLEY. So when did you learn all this?

MURIEL. Tony and I pieced together the loose ends just now in the bathroom.

ASHLEY. But what were you doing here in the first place?

MURIEL. I've been on the case since it first came up and a week ago, on my own, I found the link between Rushton and you and Mr. Deemer so I decid...

PRESCOTT. (*Offstage. Through the megaphone.*) Okay everybody, listen up! What's the concept? I notice that the birth certificate hasn't been slipped under the door yet. I advise getting going with that. I'm patient but there are limits.

ASHLEY. He's going to kill us then. He really is going to kill us. (*screams*)

TONY. (*rushing up to comfort her*) Hey, there are four of us and just one of him, so let's not panic. Okay?

GRANDPA. Okay.

TONY. But I am a little worried about fire.

ASHLEY. Oh my God, what about fire?

TONY. I don't want Prescott to try and, you know, burn the house down. Luckily it's hard to do that without some kerosene or gas or something.

ASHLEY. Oh-oh. He's got a big container full of kerosene or gas or something.

TONY. Where is it?

ASHLEY. Out by the tool shed.

(There is a loud whooosh noise and a sustained flair of orange light shining through the window.)

MURIEL. Where's that orange light coming from?

TONY. *(looking out)* Tool shed.

PRESCOTT. *(through megaphone)* See, that's exactly what we don't want happening. Big fire accident. And you people are only a birth certificate away from being absolutely free of anything like that happening to the house.

ASHLEY. I think we better give him the Birth Certificate.

TONY. No, that's the only thing keeping us safe. That's his proof you two are related to Rushton. Once he has that plus his marriage certificate he doesn't need you anymore.

ASHLEY. So what should we do?

TONY. What's upstairs?

ASHLEY. Grandpa's bedroom.

TONY. Are there any windows he could get through up there?

ASHLEY. Well there's a tree by the window on the south side. I guess he could climb the tree.

TONY. Alright we got to lock that window. *(He starts up and then stops.)* Wait a second! *(pointing to the front door)* Is there a window over *that* part of the house?

ASHLEY. Yes?

TONY. Over the front door?

ASHLEY. Right above it.

TONY. Okay here's the idea; I'm going to go up there, get the window open, and when I signal that I'm ready, I want you to put the birth certificate out the front door. Understand?

MURIEL. And then what?

TONY. When Prescott comes to pick it up, I'm going to jump him.

MURIEL. That's quite a drop.

TONY. We'll let Prescott break the fall. Where's the birth certificate?

ASHELEY, MURIEL, & GRANDPA. Closet.

TONY. Let me get it.

(He crouch walks to the closet and opens the door. Wary of being locked in again, he turns to the group and raises his hands in a "freeze" gesture.)

And I want everybody to stay exactly where they are.

(He steps into the closet, reaches in the box, and finds the certificate.)

Got it.

*(He crouch walks back out and hands the birth certificate to **ASHLEY**.)*

So when I'm in position, I'm gonna pound on the floor with my foot and then you do it. Okay?

MURIEL. So we'll just wait for your signal.

TONY. Right. One big kick on the floor. And, just in case, let's get some protection going down here.

(picking up the knife)

Muriel, got any experience using a knife before?

MURIEL. Once I filleted a fish.

TONY. *(handing her the knife)* Close enough.

(grabbing the oven cleaner from the kitchen)

And, Ashley, you use this. *(handing it to her)*

ASHLEY. Oven cleaner?

TONY. *Could* work.

*(going up to **GRANDPA** and handing him a golf club)*

And Grandpa, I want you to take this club and go into the bathroom there, and if anyone tries to break in... you know what to do.

GRANDPA. Hit balls at him.

TONY. Exactly.

*(**GRANDPA** exits and **TONY** moves towards the stairs.)*

So don't forget, when I signal, slip it under.

(He exits up the stairs.)

ASHLEY. *(as she struggles to pull off the oven cleaner cap off)* What was your name again?

MURIEL. Muriel.

ASHLEY. Muriel, I'm really scared!

MURIEL. Me too.

ASHLEY. I wish I had something for protection besides oven cleaner.

MURIEL. It's going to be okay.

ASHLEY. *(shaking a little as she still wrestles with the cap)* Muriel, I might actually be cracking up.

MURIEL. Come on now, don't worry.

ASHLEY. No, I'm serious! I'm losing it! Prescott wants to kill me!

MURIEL. We can handle it.

ASHLEY. But what about, while we're pushing the birth certificate under the front door, what if at that moment Prescott breaks in through the back door?

MURIEL. Okay well let's just get in position.

ASHLEY. Right...What position?

MURIEL. *(pointing to the back door)* You go over there and I'll go here.

*(They quickly crouch-walk to the two doors, **MURIEL** taking the birth certificate.)*

ASHLEY. *(now at the back door)* Okay good. *(intense stage whisper)* BUT THIS IS THE BACK DOOR!! Wouldn't it be better if we had the knife-person here instead of the oven-cleaner-person.

MURIEL. All right let's switch.

(They change places and as they dart quickly past each other MURIEL *hands off the birth certificate.)*

ASHLEY. *(Now at the front door. Rapidly.)* Then again, what if when Tony drops down on Prescott, Prescott overpowers Tony and then breaks through this door?! Muriel I'm so sorry but maybe I *should* be over there.

MURIEL. *(a beat)* Not a problem.

(They switch, ASHLEY *now handing back the birth certificate.)*

ASHLEY. But if he's trying to kill me wouldn...

MURIEL. Okay!

(Another switch, another birth certificate pass.)

ASHLEY. On the other ha...

MURIEL. STOP! I'm starting to like Prescott!.....Why don't we just...

(There is a loud sustained crashing noise coming from upstairs.)

ASHLEY. *(rushing over to* MURIEL*)* Oh my God! What was that!? Was that the signal?!

MURIEL. I can't tell. It seemed like an awfully long foot stomp.

ASHLEY. *(holding up the birth certificate)* So should I put this outside?!

MURIEL. I'm not sure.

ASHLEY. *(heading towards the door)* I think I should.

MURIEL. Wait!

ASHLEY. What?

MURIEL. *(Crawling over to the stairs. Calling up.)* Tony?!

(pause)

Tony!? Are you okay up there?

PRESCOTT. *(disguising his voice to sound like Tony)* Yeah, I just tripped over some golf trophies. I'm gonna to come down now.

(rushing down the stairs wearing Tony's pants and shirt)

PRESCOTT. Listen. Different strategy. I got a new plan. Everyone okay?

(crouch-dashing to the window and looking out)

Any sign of him out there?

MURIEL. We haven't seen anything.

ASHLEY. Or heard anything either. Just you doing stuff upstairs.

PRESCOTT. What's Grandpa doing?

ASHLEY. He's in there guarding I guess. I hope this all isn't too much of a strain on him.

PRESCOTT. Hey Grandpa, you okay?

GRANDPA. *(from offstage)* Okay.

MURIEL. What happened to you jumping out the window?

PRESCOTT. Changed my mind. Decided I didn't want you three vulnerable down here. Plus I came up with a better strategy.

ASHLEY. *(holding up the birth certificate)* So we're not going to put this under the door?

PRESCOTT. *(taking it)* No, too risky.

ASHLEY. Well what's the strategy?

PRESCOTT. *(peering out the window)* Okay, while I was up there I remembered something.

MURIEL. What?

PRESCOTT. *(still looking)* You're going to think it's crazy that I didn't focus on it before.

(cupping his hand to get a better view)

Damn, I wish I could see him!

MURIEL. What did you remember?

PRESCOTT. While I was upstairs it suddenly came back to me.

MURIEL. What did?

PRESCOTT. *(seeming to spot something)* Hold it. That's gotta be him! Something definitely moved out there in the bushes.

ASHLEY. Maybe it was the wind.

PRESCOTT. *(momentarily angry)* NO IT WAS NOT THE WIND! *(calmer)* It was him. That bastard is up to something. GOD HE'S CLEVER! We need to get ready. I need to get ready.

(He rushes over to **MURIEL.***)*

If you don't mind…

(He takes the knife. Then he tears back over to the window.)

Something's definitely going on with that son of a bitch. It's time to implement the strategy.

ASHLEY. And what is the strategy?

MURIEL. We're ready for the strategy.

PRESCOTT. Okay; while I was in the closet I spotted something, something amazing, and I don't know why I didn't use it right then and there.

MURIEL. *(impatiently)* WHAT WAS IT?

PRESCOTT. A box.

MURIEL. Yes?

PRESCOTT. A box of firecrackers.

ASHLEY. Really?

PRESCOTT. Big big box siting right there on the bottom shelf, stuffed with explosives.

ASHLEY. Why does Grandpa have a big box of firecrackers?

PRESCOTT. Who knows?; Fourth of July? Arnold Palmer's birthday?..the point is; he's got 'em and we can use 'em. And right now I'd like you two to snag the box and lug it over here while I stand guard.

MURIEL. You want us to bring you the firecrackers.

PRESCOTT. Right.

MURIEL. .....Okay.

(nodding towards closet)

And they're right in there?

PRESCOTT. Yes.

MURIEL. I'm not too thrilled about going into the closet again but...

(MURIEL and ASHLEY go to the closet and hesitantly look in, then both of them step inside. After a moment...)

I'm afraid I don't see any firecrackers.

ASHLEY. Me either. Tony, we don't see any firecrackers.

PRESCOTT. *(as he leaves the window and heads to the closet)* Come on; it's a huge box down there on the bottom shelf. You can't miss it.

ASHLEY. What bottom shelf?

PRESCOTT. The bottom shelf that's.... *(as he slams the door shut)* on the bottom!!

(When ASHLEY and MURIEL push on the door he grabs a golf club and wedges it across.)

MURIEL. *(from inside)* Tony! Tony! Why did you close the door?

ASHLEY. Tony, I think you should open the door.

PRESCOTT. Not right now thanks.

(ASHLEY and MURIEL start pounding at the closet.)

Cut that out!

ASHLEY. *(from inside)* Oh my God; PRESCOTT!

(There is frantic pounding from the closet.)

PRESCOTT. Stop it!! *(It stops.)* Any more noise and that's it! I mean it! Understand! *(looking around)* What's Grandpa doing? *(calling out)* Grandpa!! Grandpa!!

GRANDPA. *(from the bathroom)* Yo.

PRESCOTT. Grandpa, you okay in there?

GRANDPA. What's that?

PRESCOTT. Is everything okay?

GRANDPA. One more time?

PRESCOTT. Grandpa, listen, I'm going to go outside for a minute now, you understand.

GRANDPA. I can't hear you.

PRESCOTT. I said I'm going to go get the can of odorless undectable kerosene and then I'm going to bring it back inside and splash it throughout the house so that I can burn you all to death. Is that okay?

GRANDPA. Okay in here!

PRESCOTT. Good, I'll be right back.

*(He goes out the front door. After a moment, **GRANDPA** comes out of the bathroom and looks around.)*

GRANDPA. *(muttering to himself)* I'm not *that* deaf.

*(He goes over to where the golf ball is on the tee and gets in position for Prescott's return. **PRESCOTT**, carrying the kerosene can and the gun, opens the door and steps inside. He sees **GRANDPA**.)*

PRESCOTT. Well Grandpa, what are you doing? Practicing a little?

GRANDPA. Hold it now.

PRESCOTT. I'd just as soon you didn't hit that golf ball in my direction if it's all the same to you.

GRANDPA. Just a second.

(He pulls his arms back to begin his stroke.)

PRESCOTT. I mean it!!

*(aiming the gun at **GRANDPA**)*

Grandpa, put the club down!

GRANDPA. You know what? This is feeling a little better.

PRESCOTT. Drop it or I really will shoot!

GRANDPA. Get ready now, here we go!

(They are frozen for a moment as they each aim at each other.)

(The lights go out and a shot is heard.)

(extended blackout)

(As the lights come up; it's morning, birds are chirping and **ASHLEY** *[crying a little] is waving goodbye out the front door.)*

ASHLEY. *(calling out)* Okay, well, thanks again, Officer Sutcliff, and thank you, Officer Woodard. I really appreciate it. *(She sniffles.)* Thank you all so very much.

(MURIEL *comes in from the backdoor.)*

MURIEL. Hey Ashley, it's okay!

(She goes up to her and puts her arm on **ASHLEY***'s shoulder. She waves out the door as she closes it. Calling out.)*

Yes, thank you, Officers. We're really grateful for everything you did. Bye.

ASHLEY. Muriel! *(more sobbing)*

MURIEL. This has been such a terrible time for you.

ASHLEY. I know. I know. I just can't seem to calm down about it. *(She weeps some more.)*

MURIEL. *(taking her in her arms)* Here, let's just let it all out. That's right. Come on. You've been through an awful lot.

ASHLEY. So have you.

MURIEL. I know, but it's not really the same. I mean you've had such a personal loss.

ASHLEY. You can't imagine. On so many levels. I just can't stop thinking about...him. He had such a quality. *(sniffles)* So sweet. So good natured.

MURIEL. I know.

ASHLEY. I mean, oh my God; what a way to go!

MURIEL. At least it was quick.

ASHLEY. You don't think he suffered?

MURIEL. No. Not at all.

(ASHLEY *lets out a mournful cry and sobs some more.)*

ASHLEY. Oh I feel so bad for *(sobbing loudly)* Grandpa!

GRANDPA. *(coming out of the bathroom)* Yo.

MURIEL. (to **ASHLEY***)* It's okay.

GRANDPA. Did somebody call me?

MURIEL. No, we were just expressing our grief about the bird.

GRANDPA. What's that?

MURIEL. We're mourning.

GRANDPA. Sorry?

MURIEL. MOURNING.

GRANDPA. Morning. Did those officers leave?

ASHLEY. Just now. They wanted me to tell you again what an amazing feat you performed.

GRANDPA. I don't know, if I'd done it a little different maybe Prescott wouldn't have taken that wild shot and hit Freckles.

MURIEL. Well, they said it was a phenomenal achievement.

GRANDPA. Oh my gosh, wasn't all that great. You know; just a matter of setting up right, getting focused, shifting the weight, keeping my eye on the ball, and then just smashing the Hell out of it. I got to say though, I'm pretty exited to get my stroke back. *(to MURIEL)* Say, you don't play golf do you?

MURIEL. No sorry.

GRANDPA. Too bad.

ASHLEY. The officer said that they're going to take Tony back up to Macon, and after he gets treated at the hospital they'll try and get him released from custody right away.

GRANDPA. *(going to sit on the couch)* Well, good for him. So they don't think that head wound he got upstairs is so bad?

ASHLEY. No, it just knocked him out. Apparently there wasn't any significant damage. When he gets out he can go right back to horse tooth filing.

MURIEL. And what are you going to do?

ASHLEY. What do you mean?

MURIEL. You are now a very rich woman.

ASHLEY. Oh right, I forgot.

MURIEL. You can do anything you want.

ASHLEY. Right now what I'd like to do is set up an organization that could help birds and…other animals like maybe, I don't know, horses.

MURIEL. And what about you, Mr. Deemer? What are you going to do with all your money?

GRANDPA. Well, let me think. *(pause)* You know what I'd really like to do?

MURIEL. What?

GRANDPA. Get boys and girls that are disadvantaged and underprivileged who don't have much to look forward to and then teach them to play golf.

MURIEL. I think that's a wonderful idea. Listen, if you need a lawyer to assist you in setting up something like that, here's where you can reach me. *(giving him her card)*

GRANDPA. Why, thank you.

ASHLEY. Grandpa, can I use your car?

GRANDPA. Sure where you going?

ASHLEY. I'm going to drive up to Macon.

GRANDPA. What for?

ASHLEY. I just want to hang out and see if Tony, you know, needs anything.

GRANDPA. Do you want me to come with you?

ASHLEY. No, I think I should do this on my own. Let me go get my stuff. *(She exits up the stairs.)*

MURIEL. Mr. Deemer, I like the idea of setting up a foundation. I think that's such a good use of your capital. And I really mean it, if you like, I'd be more than happy to assist you in getting it going.

GRANDPA. Well, I can use all the assistance I can get.

MURIEL. 'Cause I would love to participate in such a venture.

GRANDPA. What's that?

MURIEL. I WANT TO HELP YOU.

GRANDPA. GOOD.

MURIEL. And I think I can help you quite a bit.

GRANDPA. I'm sure.

MURIEL. *(joining him on the couch)* I need to set things up so that you're not legally vulnerable...

GRANDPA. We don't want that.

MURIEL. Mr. Deemer, I have a feeling that we can work together.

GRANDPA. *(pleasantly)* I bet you're right.

MURIEL. You and I.

GRANDPA. Probably.

MURIEL. If I may say so I have the impression that we might make an effective team..

GRANDPA. Right...who?

MURIEL. You and I. Mr. Deemer, your life is about to go through some radical changes and nothing would please me more than to help make those changes as positive as I can. I realize we haven't known each other very long but I feel that my legal expertise coupled with the fact that we've been through some highly charged life experiences together should create a professional and, if I may say so, personal rapport that could help make your upcoming life transitions much more comfortable. *(meaningfully)* In fact, as far as you and I are concerned, I think it all could be made very comfortable. *(pause)* What do you think of that?

GRANDPA. *(maintaining his pleasant demeanor, picking up the megaphone)* Excuse me for a second. I need to tell Ashley something. *(going to the stairs and aiming the megaphone up them)* SAND TRAP!!!

(curtain)

A NOTE ON PLAYING
TONY AND PRESCOTT

Tony and Prescott (played, of course, by the same actor) should exhibit distinctive personalities. Tony is more earnest and deliberate and has a stronger southern accent, Prescott has a more urban flair – speaks more rapidly, maybe a little higher pitched. There might also be physical movement differences between the two and maybe a hair difference as well; Tony's hair, say, might stick up, Prescott's lie flat.

In addition: the play works best if the audience doesn't know in advance that Tony looks just like Prescott. To help with that, the program and advertizing might conceal the double/role aspect with a fictitious actor's name. Further, at the opening, when the cast takes their places, if a complete black out can't be achieved–Tony might get behind the closet door via a secret opening in the flat.

COSTUMES

GRANDPA - Loose, well-worn golf attire.

MURIEL - Summer-weight business suit.

ASHLEY - Athletic light cruise-wear.

TONY - First seen in roughed-up orange prison jumpsuit. While in the closet, changes into a black shirt and Grandpa's loud plaid pants (Pants need to be easy to get in and out of – maybe a velcro fly-away construction).

PRESCOTT - Casual pants and a black polo shirt (shirt needs to look enough like Tony's so Grandpa won't notice the difference).

PROPS

Act One
"Welcome Newlyweds" banner, golf club, golf balls, golf floor tee, little hearing aid, Muriel's purse, Muriel's large colorful nail file (needs to be recognizable for the second act break out), birdcage, bird, telephone with cut cord, megaphone, wedding announcement clipping in frame, Ashley's purse, Ashley's travel bag, eye glasses for Ashley, hand gun, ping pong paddle, large "ice tea" container (needs to be somewhat bigger than a typical ice tea container).

Act Two
Oranges, carving knife, juice glasses, pitcher, vacuum cleaner with long hose and nozzles, duct tape, kitchen towel, oven cleaner spray can, birth certificate, business card for Muriel.

SOUND EFFECTS

Bird tweeting, car arriving, gas flow hiss, tool shed igniting (sound and visual), Prescott talking through megaphone (on tape), onstage gun-shot.

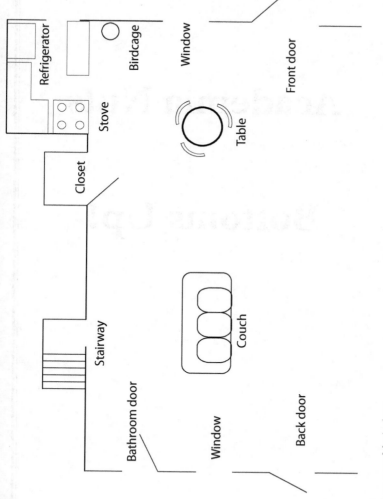

Image appears courtesy of the Author

Also by
Gregg Kreutz...

Academia Nuts

Bottoms Up!

OTHER TITLES AVAILABLE FROM SAMUEL FRENCH

BOTTOMS UP!

Gregg Kreutz

Farce / 6m, 3f / Multiple Sets

"Suitcase, suitcase, who's got the suitcase?" is the urgent question in this hilarious farce set in a Caribbean hotel. One composite set represents the hotel's lobby, elevator, and second floor. The comedy charts the confusion that occurs when June, an earnest aerobics instructor, unknowingly acquires the cash filled suitcase of two money launderers from Cleveland. Their attempts to retrieve it cause a soft core movie director to mistake June for the next star of his basement budget production "Tan All Over." Then he discovers the money and joins the convoluted efforts to get the suitcase. Interference is provided by his former star who is now an outraged moralist, a nervous chemistry instructor visiting the island under duress, the hotel owner and her sticky-fingered nephew. Wild chases, bizarre disguises, and the silliest looking aerobics dance ever make this a truly riotous farce.

CPSIA information can be obtained
at www.ICGtesting.com
Printed in the USA
FSHW012115011118
53495FS